THE ALIEN BODYGUARD

Interspecies Alliances Book 2

ERYN IVERS

Chapter One

OLIVER TURNER JERKED awake with a gasp and remembered terror, his own screams and the disappointed tone of his father echoing in his head. It took just a moment for his heart rate to slow back down, and then he curled his lip in disgust.

Typical.

He would have a damn dream tonight, of all nights.

He threw off his sheets, and his stomach rolled at the cold sweat-soaked fabric sticking to his skin. He tore himself out with a grunt, then made for his bathroom. His shirt and underwear fell onto the floor with a squelch that made him cringe as he peeled them off on his way, leaving a trail of damp clothes behind him.

Stepping onto the cold tile of the shower, he slammed his hand on the button. Sweet relief finally shuddered through him as the hot water sprayed onto him and sluiced away the slick remnants of his nightmare.

Calmed by the water beating down on his shoulders, Oliver leaned his head against the wall of the shower and sighed. So much for nine hours of sleep before the big day.

He could see Dominic's eager sneer already—the one he tried to hide, but that always peeked through when he thought he was going to win. But only ever when their father's back was turned.

Oliver scoffed to himself. It wasn't a *big* day—it was the *first* day. First days were all about first impressions, and he could make a striking first impression in his sleep. That's why he'd been chosen for this job and why Dominic had never had a shot at it, even if he had been enjoying Oliver's pedestal for the last several years.

With that thought, Oliver straightened and stretched, truly awake now and resigned to staying that way. He'd use the extra time to deeply consider what to wear.

He lathered some of his soap onto his silk washcloth and paused when the characteristic smell of earth lavender and pure wealth didn't hit as clearly as it usually did. Then he sighed as he remembered. He'd had his favorite soap reformulated to suit klah'eel olfactory senses. The manufacturer had assured him it still smelled exactly the same—and when Oliver pressed his nose close to the washcloth, he could confirm that it did—but it was barely detectable to a human and wouldn't overpower a klah'eel.

It wouldn't do to go into serious contract negotiations smelling like potpourri, but it was still a little disappointing.

After showering, he dried and toweled his blond hair and then styled it into something sleek and refined while it was still damp. Returning to the room, he steeled himself before stripping off the wet sheets, then threw them into the hamper in the corner.

That done, Oliver threw open the doors of his closet and smiled at the contents with his hands on his bare hips. Now to decide what of his obscenely expensive and perfectly tailored wardrobe would be best suited to making an entrance into the Klah'Eel empire and the state of Northern Tava.

CAPTAIN MAL'IK OPENED HIS EYES, perfectly awake and perfectly aware. No threats. Not an item out of place. He sat up, put his feet on the ground, and rolled his shoulders—his joints creaking more than they used to but not feeling any stiffer.

The Turner ship landed in three hours. He expected their arrival and even the welcoming banquet to be a quiet affair from a security standpoint. The humans' own security force would still be present, as they had insisted—correctly—that without extra precautions, it would be the most obvious time to strike. The job would get more interesting after they left, entrusting the security of their VIP to the Klah'Eel as a show of goodwill.

But expectations for quiet were not excuses for laziness. Mal'ik picked up the tablet from his nightstand and scrolled through last night's reports. Nothing. Good.

He set the tablet aside and moved through his morning routine. Shower. Polish his teeth and his tusks. Rub lotion on the stump of his right shoulder and around the prosthetic input ports. Wipe the night's dust off his right arm, and then click it into place. Allow the hiss of pain to escape, since there was no one around to hear, as the artificial nerves connected with the remaining ones in his shoulder. Tighten the harness that kept his arm in place around his chest.

Make his bed. Dress in uniform. Check his gatlung. Grab his bags. Leave.

The population of the political compound on which he and dozens of other security and service personnel lived

3

had swelled to the low hundreds for these negotiations with and about the Turner family, and the halls and arcades bustled with people. Mal'ik passed rooms in the guest quarters still being turned out and meeting rooms being aired. The estate hadn't been so busy since the war, and not for as long as Mal'ik had been posted at it.

He found his temporary accommodations in the guest wing—so much nicer than his living accommodations in the security wing—dropped off his bags, then made for the dining hall to meet with his security team.

When Mal'ik arrived, a familiar, muscular klah'eel woman was chewing on a roll.

He smiled. "Lar'a."

Lar'a swallowed her mouthful and grinned. She stood up and spread her arms. "Old man!"

Mal'ik let himself be pulled into a hug and returned it, inhaling deeply. The younger woman smelled calm, confident, content. "You smell well."

Lar'a let him go and leaned against the table with her mug of klak. "I am well. Still with Serihk."

Mal'ik poured himself a mug. "He's still a good employer?"

Lar'a had left Mal'ik's Gat'Raph unit almost fifteen years ago to take a position as the Qeshian Emissary's personal bodyguard. She had never looked back.

"The very best, as usual." Lar'a took a swig of her klak and tilted her mug at him. "On that topic, we've got a new human consultant staying with us, and he needs his own bodyguard. I was hoping you could refer someone."

Mal'ik nodded. "Send me some information. I'll send you some names."

"Will do. He—"

"Lar'a, you stranger!" Patrick strode through the door, his blue eyes bright, and grabbed Lar'a into a hug. "What the hell are you doing here? This is a classified meeting, you know."

"So we should be kicking out the hangers-on like you then?" Lar'a scoffed and returned the hug but used her superior height to rub her knuckles into Patrick's salt-and-pepper hair.

"Hangers-on nothing." Patrick disengaged and went for the breakfast rolls. He jerked his head at Mal'ik. "This old man would be lost without me."

Mal'ik indulged him with a smile and didn't dispute. He and Patrick had been fighting together since the Klah'Eel invasion of Tava, when Patrick had joined the Klah'Eel side despite being human. He'd always been a Klah'Eel citizen, and he had chosen loyalty to his country over loyalty to his species. Now, he had been Mal'ik's right-hand man for many years.

A slightly built and younger klah'eel woman with black hair in thick braids down her back came in quietly behind Patrick. She nodded at Lar'a. "Hello. I don't believe we've met."

"Teav, this is Lar'a." Mal'ik stepped between them to make the proper introductions. "She's the bodyguard of the Qeshian Emissary Serihk and has her own security concerns and insights. She's an excellent security profes-sional, and she'll be in constant contact with us during the negotiations. Lar'a, this is Teav, our brilliant intelligence expert."

Lar'a lifted her mug in a highly informal salute.

Teav's eyebrow twitched. "Pleased to meet you."

"And you."

Traces of distrust and wariness wafted off them both, but Mal'ik ignored it. They were security experts. He would have been concerned about their fitness for duty if they'd taken to each other immediately.

He sat at the head of the table and waved for them all to join him. "Let's get this started. The Turner ship will be here soon. What do I need to know?"

Patrick spoke first, his face tight, accentuating the lines around his lips. "Teav. Tell him what you told me."

Teav's jaw flexed as she gritted her teeth. "I don't have anything."

Lar'a's eyes narrowed. "What?"

"I don't have anything," Teav repeated. Her eyes cut briefly to Lar'a before settling on Mal'ik. "The Resistance is quiet. There was chatter about hitting a trading post tens of kilometers from Ralscoln, but that was a transparent decoy."

"You haven't heard anything about this summit?" Mal'ik tightened the grip of his flesh hand around the warm ceramic mug.

"No. And we know they're interested in it."

"You bet they are." Lar'a leaned back and crossed her arms. "They care a hell of a lot more about this than some trading post in the Southern Tava hinterlands."

"I know," Teav shot back on just the right side of rude. "Deception experts they are not, but they clearly know how to shut up when they need to."

Mal'ik frowned. "Have you heard anything about the torvar?"

The table went quiet.

Lar'a and Patrick sat up a little straighter.

Teav deflated. "No," she admitted. "The last we heard, he'd sabotaged a power plant just south of Ralscoln. No rumors since then."

Patrick growled. "Fuck."

Lar'a rubbed a thumb over her eyebrow horns and grimaced. "I hate those goddamn worms."

Mal'ik kept his face neutral and nodded slowly. "It is

what it is. It will be a feat for him to get through our entrance scans."

"He's gotten through plenty before," Patrick pointed out.

"He's gotten through half-assed and corrupt entry points in Southern Tava." Lar'a wrinkled her nose. "This is a different game."

Mal'ik could smell the anxiety on her, though. If the klah'eel had ever had a natural predator, it was the torvar. It didn't matter that they had an advanced space-faring civilization now; the thought of the parasite still flicked on an instinctual fear switch in the back of their minds.

"Just because I haven't heard anything from the Resistance a hemisphere away doesn't mean I won't hear anything if they start making moves here," Teav reminded them, lifting her chin. "We won't be caught completely off guard."

"No, we won't." Mal'ik stood, and the other three followed. "Patrick, double the scans for incoming ships. Teav, I want you to focus on the Resistance. I'm no longer worried about any other factions."

"Are you sure?" Lar'a asked before they could disperse. "Our human consultant says there are plenty of Human factions that might have a vested interest in seeing the Turner family fail here."

Teav nodded slowly. "I doubt any of them, criminal or otherwise, would act directly, but they might be happy to foot the Resistance's bill. I'll put one of my men on investigating finances."

"Good." Mal'ik looked around at them. "Anything else?"

"No, sir," Teav said with a straight back.

Patrick and Lar'a both shook their heads.

Mal'ik nodded once. "Alright. Dismissed. The Turner ship is landing within the hour."

Patrick fell into step beside Mal'ik as they walked to the landing bay. He seemed to have shaken off the stress of the meeting, and he gave Mal'ik a little smirk. "You ready for this?"

"Why wouldn't I be?"

"You haven't done close protection in a while."

Mal'ik scowled. "It's my specialty."

"*Was* your specialty," Patrick corrected. "You've been a captain for years now."

"I still am. *Your* captain, in fact." Mal'ik gave him a stern look from his superior height, but Patrick smirked again.

"And *his* nursemaid."

It was considered an honor to have the best—often interpreted as the highest-ranking—security professional assigned to the most important guest. An honor for the guard or for the guest, Mal'ik couldn't say, but it was only through promising to assign Mal'ik that the Klah'Eel had gotten Turner's bodyguard to agree to leave the planet during the negotiations.

Patrick was still watching him, and Mal'ik almost rolled his eyes, as though they were still young men. "I'll be fine."

"I hear he's a pain in the ass."

Mal'ik snorted. "They always are."

They arrived at the landing bay—the big, audacious one specifically for use by guests that the government wanted to impress—and took their place around the perimeter of the group that had gathered. The Klah'Eel government and business heads and their entourages had organized themselves by importance and power.

Mal'ik touched his earpiece. "Everyone in position?"

The squad leaders sounded off in the affirmative.

"Good," he said. "Keep your eyes on the crowd, the entrances, and the perimeter."

Soon, the flare of an incoming ship entering the atmosphere appeared in the sky, and then a sleek silver transport ship sped toward them. Mal'ik raised an eyebrow. The ship was quiet and fast and shone in the sun. The posturing had already started then.

But the ship—as nice as it was—was nothing compared to the human man that first appeared down the gangway.

Mal'ik's first thought was that it was foolish and completely against protocol to allow an assignment first through a doorway. He should be flanked. A bodyguard in front and a bodyguard behind at least.

Mal'ik's second thought was that he was breathtaking. His hair caught the sun like gold; the pure white of his clothing reflected the light blindingly. He held himself straight and tall and swept down the gangway as though alighting from a throne. Mal'ik swallowed against his suddenly too-tight collar.

And Mal'ik's third thought was to realize that the first two were very connected. This man knew how to make an entrance, and he wasn't going to let a silly thing like his own security and the duties of his bodyguards ruin that for him.

He *was* going to be a pain in the ass, but Mal'ik's lips wanted to smile at the confident audacity of it.

"Have fun," Patrick murmured next to him with a tilt to his eyebrows that indicated his mind had gone through at least some of the same thoughts.

"Don't be so quick to mock," Mal'ik warned him. "Who do you think is going to have to help me when he's too much to handle?"

"Well, I'm going to be busy coordinating the rest of this operation," Patrick said. "So it won't be me."

"Oh yes it will."

THE INTRODUCTIONS and the banquet were as tedious and exhausting as Oliver had expected them to be: full of pomp and posturing, which Oliver was very good at but didn't find particularly engaging. He'd identified the major players and adjusted his mental dossiers as needed so that he could adjust the actual ones on his data tablet when he got to his rooms. Before official talks began, he'd arranged one-on-one meetings for tomorrow with potential allies and adversaries. Overall, it had all gone as planned, and he was quite ready to test out his accommodations and scrub off the horrible scent-neutralizing cream smeared all over his pulse points, but there was one thing left to do.

"I've been assured he's the very best," Garin told him for at least the third time as he walked Oliver to his rooms.

"I'm sure he is," Oliver said.

"You know your father would never allow anything else."

"I know."

Kevin Garin had been Oliver's bodyguard for six years now—after his first bodyguard had been killed in action—and he was clearly more upset at the prospect of leaving Oliver than Oliver was. This was perfectly reasonable, considering that Garin would lose an extremely lucrative protection contract if Oliver were to die.

"We'll be just in the orbital station," Garin continued. "Technically only a transport ship away. I can be down in hours if you request me."

Oliver stopped and turned to face Garin. "Which I will not because it would be a terrible idea. It's bad enough you'll be on that station."

Garin pressed his lips together in that disapproving thin line that never gave Oliver any more patience. They had discussed this. At length. The Klah'Eel were a warrior empire above all else, and they found the idea that they couldn't protect their own guests supremely offensive. It was not an offense Oliver wanted to give.

"Like you said, he's the best." Oliver resumed walking and waved a hand over his shoulder. "Now let's just meet him so I can go to bed."

Garin followed and didn't try to reassure him again. They walked through the arcades of the estate's guest wing, the night air surprisingly pleasant on Oliver's skin. Northern Tava was notoriously hot, but Oliver had always hated being cold, so maybe the fact that so many of the walkways were open to the air wasn't so b—

Oliver stopped dead when he rounded a corner.

He had met klah'eel before this trip, and he had met even more today. He'd assumed he'd acclimated to their size, but the klah'eel man standing in front of him now still brought him up short. The man stood outside of a door practically at attention. He was facing the wall across from him and not the hall they'd just come from, so Oliver got a good look at his profile: strong jaw, full lips resting on polished tusks, heavy brow, a prominent and defined nose. Oliver's eyes trailed of their own volition down the corded muscle of his neck and the bulging muscle of his bare arms—

Arm, he mentally corrected with a shock as the klah'eel man turned to face them. His left arm had bulging muscles, but his right was mechanical, with wires and pistons and plating disappearing under the fabric of his sleeveless uniform shirt. And only the left side of his lips was full; the right was twisted up in the scar tissue that ran down that side of his face.

Oliver met the man's orange eyes and felt a sudden—strong, shocking, unprecedented, and wholly inappropriate—wave of arousal. The man's nostrils flared, and Oliver instantly changed his mind about the scent-neutralizing cream still heavy on his skin. It was a wonderful godsend, and he never wanted to take it off. The dirty place his mind had skittered to before he could pull it back did *not* need to be advertised by his pheromones.

"Captain Mal'ik." Garin held his hand out to the arresting man, and he took it in a firm grip. "I'm Kevin Garin. We've spoken over transmission."

"Right." Captain Mal'ik nodded as he shook Garin's hand. "Good to meet you." He turned those intense eyes back to Oliver, and Oliver lifted his chin and pulled his shoulders back before his body language could show anything but cool indifference. "Oliver Turner?"

"Yes." Oliver nodded and did not extend his hand. "I understand you'll be providing my close protection during these talks?"

"That's correct." Captain Mal'ik's voice was deep and rumbling, and Oliver felt it in the center of his chest. He fought the urge to swoon and then to scowl. He shouldn't be feeling anyone's voice that deep inside him.

"Wonderful. Well, I assume you've coordinated with Garin, and now I've been handed off, and we've been acquainted." Oliver flapped his hands between them and then quickly dropped them back down to his sides before he could do something else just as stupid with them. "So if there's nothing else, I'm assuming there's a bed somewhere behind that door you're standing in front of that I'd really rather like to be acquainted with next."

Oliver wanted to step around the man and get going, but he really was standing right in front of it. Oliver might actually have to touch him to get to it, and he was certainly not going to do that.

"Do you need anything before I leave?" Garin asked.

Oliver turned to him and sighed loudly. "No, Garin, I do not. Do *you* need anything before you leave?"

Garin's lips thinned again. "No."

"I'll take it from here," Mal'ik said in that deep, slow voice.

Garin glanced at him, nodded, and then had the gall to shrug. "Right. Good luck." Then he turned on his heel and left.

Oliver supposed another man might have been kinder to Garin. But another man might have been fooled into thinking Garin was genuinely concerned with Oliver's wellbeing, and Oliver was not so foolish.

Oliver turned back to this Captain Mal'ik and tried not to be intimidated by how he had to tilt his chin up to look at him. "Great. And do *you* need anything before I go to sleep?"

"Yes," Mal'ik replied, and he turned to the door and input its code.

Oliver's breath caught in his throat. His mind jumped out of reality and straight into a fantasy in which what Mal'ik needed was Oliver, naked on the bed, writhing in ecstasy as Mal'ik pinned him beneath all of those muscles and watched him with those electric orange eyes.

"I want to sweep the rooms before I leave."

Right. Of course. That was infinitely more reasonable. Back to reality for him. "Well, make it quick."

Oliver followed Mal'ik into the rooms, skirting around him as soon as he could to get a look at his accommodations. They were appropriately sumptuous if a little uninspired. Oliver had no intention of giving up his accustomed luxuries while away, and he was glad he wouldn't have to make a fuss about it.

Looking around, he wouldn't say the decorator was anything special, but they had taste. A klah'eel's taste, certainly. Things were a bit more brutalist than the current human fashion, but Oliver could appreciate the clean lines and lack of clutter. And there was still plenty of softness to be found in the window coverings and the seating, enough to convince Oliver that the bed would meet his standards.

He stayed put in the first room, an entertaining area with a low table, a couch, and a couple of chairs, with his hands on his hips as he watched Mal'ik work. The klah'eel swept his gaze over the room, nostrils flaring as he scented it, taking in the room on another plane of observation that Oliver could barely understand.

Then he strode to the room on the left, a small study, and peered under the desk and opened the cabinets. Even his almost blank, focused expression was intense, and Oliver found himself shifting and swallowing as he watched the man stride past him again to the door on the right.

That must be the bedroom, so Oliver followed him in. His things had been unpacked and arranged, and when Mal'ik opened the closet, Oliver saw his extensive wardrobe hanging neatly.

Mal'ik paused there, standing in front of the open closet. Oliver was behind him, watching his broad back, but he felt oddly exposed and had a sudden desire to slam the doors shut and hide away whatever it was Mal'ik was observing in there.

He crossed his arms over his chest and affected a dry tone that impressed even himself with how real it sounded. "Is there an assassin hiding among my suits then?"

"No," Mal'ik said simply, either not irritated by Oliver's

tone or good at hiding it. He closed the doors and then moved across the bedroom to the other door, opening it to reveal a large bathroom. Even larger than the one on Oliver's personal ship, and he'd had that one custom built.

But it was still just a bathroom, and after a moment, Mal'ik reemerged. "You're clear."

"Thank heavens," Oliver deadpanned.

Mal'ik walked toward him—Oliver overcame the instinctual response to step back and kept his arms crossed —and stopped in front of him. "My room is across the hall," he said. "There will be two guards posted outside your door all night. I'll return in the morning. Sleep well."

Oliver nodded crisply, and Mal'ik walked around him to leave the room. Oliver listened to his heavy footsteps crossing the first room, the door opening, and then the door closing. He didn't realize he'd been holding his breath until it came out in a deep, shuddering sigh.

Chapter Two

MAL'IK MUST HAVE SMELLED him wrong.

The scent cream must have reacted poorly to the changes in atmosphere between the station and the planet and skewed the signals. That or Mal'ik's nose was playing tricks on him.

It had just been a whiff.

Or two, rather. One as the human had followed him into the rooms and another as Mal'ik had passed him while he left. Two snatches of a base, earthy scent that had made Mal'ik's blood run hot and thrum with promise.

A growl rumbled in Mal'ik's chest as he recalled it.

It had to have been wrong.

The scent that had hit Mal'ik's nose when he'd opened the closet, though, had been impossible to miss. Fresh air. Sunshine. Cleanliness. Like the smell of the bedsheets he had helped his mother hang up to dry in the summers of his childhood in Klah. For a moment, he hadn't been able to move, and it was a damn good thing there *hadn't* been an assassin in there.

Mal'ik shook his head to dislodge the thoughts. That

the man smelled as nice as he looked, if not nicer, was not his concern.

A few minutes later, the night guards arrived. He told them to wake him for any concerns and then entered the door to his own temporary rooms across the hall. They were much smaller than the ones the important people were put up in but plenty comfortable. A single room with a small table, a couch, a bed, and a small attached bathroom.

He'd only stepped in long enough to drop off his bags this morning, and now he set about unpacking them. He hadn't packed much, as he wouldn't need much. Close protection operations would limit his alone time to an hour before bed, sleeping, and an hour after. If there was an incident, he would get even less.

Dropping off his tusk polish and showering supplies in the bathroom, he caught himself staring at his scar in the mirror over the sink and scowled. He hadn't been concerned about his scar in years. What did it matter if it gnarled up half his face? It was proof that he had put his body and his life on the line for his duty. Besides, his job was to watch Turner, not the other way around. Turner didn't need to look at it.

Not that it mattered if he did look at it. Or what he thought of it. Or if it made him uncomfortable.

Mal'ik turned his back on the mirror as he brushed his teeth, turning around only long enough to spit, and then he stalked back into his room. He removed his prosthetic, stripped off his clothes, turned off his light, and fell into bed and an almost instant, dreamless slumber.

In eight hours precisely, he woke up.

He turned on his light, brushed his teeth, put on his prosthetic, made his bed, put on his clothes, slung his gatlung over his shoulder, and opened his door.

He nodded in greeting to the second-shift night guards. "Anything to report?"

"No, sir. All quiet."

"Good. Get some rest."

Once they left, Mal'ik knocked on Turner's door. "It's Mal'ik. I'm coming in."

Without waiting for a response, Mal'ik unlocked the door and stepped inside. The living room was empty and exactly as Mal'ik had left it. The study was also untouched. He heard running water and movement coming from the bedroom and its bathroom.

"What's the point of knocking if you just barge in anyway?" Turner called out from the other room. "Humans consider that rude, you know. In fact, *I* consider that rude."

The point of knocking was to give the assignment a moment to escape embarrassment if they were without clothes or in some other compromising position. The point of not waiting was to take away any moment of escape from any potential hostile. But Mal'ik didn't think Turner really cared about the reasons, so he kept quiet.

"I'm not done yet, so sit down or something. I can hear you hovering from here," Turner called again, and Mal'ik heard what sounded like bare feet on tile and the closet door opening. His mind suddenly supplied the image of Turner—smooth, creamy bare skin on display and his hair still dripping—standing in front of his collection of clothes, smelling and looking like sunlight.

He bared his teeth and shoved the image away.

After a moment, the closet doors squeaked shut and booted footsteps approached the bedroom door. Turner stepped out, fully clothed but still looking like sunlight, his hair slicked back from his high cheekbones and one blond brow cocked.

"Still standing, I see. That's lovely and not awkward at all."

Mal'ik didn't reply, his brain still wrestling with the discomfort of having his eyes perceive something that his nose could not. A complete olfactory void occupied the place where Turner stood, redolent in his pristine white-and-gold trimmed pants and a collared shirt. Nothing to scent at all. He had gone very heavy on the scent-neutral-izing cream. Looking at Turner's throat, Mal'ik saw swirls over his pulse points where he had lain it on too thick for it to be absorbed.

Mal'ik saw a flash of movement and looked back up at Turner's face just in time to see the tip of his pink tongue swipe over his lower lip. But before Mal'ik could get to his hazel eyes, Turner swept into motion and strode past him.

"Let's go then." Turner yanked the door open before Mal'ik could stop him and remind him of proper protec-tion protocol. "I'm hungry, and I hate to play politics on an empty stomach."

Turner didn't rebel against protocol again, and for the rest of the morning and through lunch, the operation fell into the regular routines of a close protection assignment. It was even duller than the operations Mal'ik used to run back when he'd been protecting politicians and aid workers in Southern Tava during the occupation.

He mostly watched Turner have tea parties with the upper crust of Klah'Eel society. Mal'ik wasn't such a musclebound fool that he didn't understand what was happening, though. Turner and each official he spoke to were probing each other, feeling each other out, deciding weaknesses, strengths, and whether they were allies or adversaries.

Turner might be finding some allies, Mal'ik couldn't say, but he certainly wasn't finding any friends. The man found fault with everything, and when he didn't find an explicit fault, he certainly implied it had one. The tea was too sweet or not sweet enough. The comfort of the chairs would do, he supposed. Was this the *usual* spread of delicacies he could expect at a diplomat's private lunch then?

Mal'ik almost laughed at the waves of baffled indignation rolling off their hosts. Klah'Eel didn't complain, and they didn't know what to do with someone who did.

"And is that how your young are educated then? *All* of them?" Turner asked in the same tone he had asked if that was really how they arranged their silverware. He was meeting with the education minister now, charged with educating the next generation of Klah'Eel citizens, whether klah'eel, human, or other. It was the first time Mal'ik had heard that scathing tone applied to something of consequence.

"Yes, of course." The minister drew himself up. "All of them. We don't discriminate by species here."

"That's admirable, I'm sure, but you do realize they're not all the same person, don't you?" Turner raised an eyebrow and managed to tilt his head in such a way that he looked down his nose at the much larger man. "You're treating them like cardboard cutouts. You can't expect to get the same outputs from a single process with different inputs. I'm no scientist, but even I know that."

The minister gaped for a moment, but Turner was already continuing.

"And why would you even want to?" he asked, clearly rhetorically. "A society takes all sorts to run properly. If you were only providing one, I'd say you were failing."

He hadn't exactly said the minister *wasn't* failing, and judging by the pungent odor that filled the room, the minister had noticed that. Turner didn't so much as flick his nose, his weak human sense completely oblivious. It didn't take a klah'eel's nose to see the minister's thunderous brows, though, and Turner didn't seem bothered by that either.

Mal'ik almost smiled.

"You raise very valid points." The minister almost managed to sound genuine. "I'm sure we'll have time to discuss them at length during the education meetings."

"Yes, I'm sure." Turner sipped the tea he had declared too sweet. "I look forward to it."

Mal'ik had nothing to do but keep an eye on the perimeter, receive reports from his team—all clear—and watch Turner eviscerate everything around him for the whole day, until Turner's last meeting with Governor Tesh of Southern Tava.

Turner stayed quiet and rigid as they walked to the meeting. He didn't even comment on the small puddle of standing water from that afternoon's rain that had gathered around one of the pillars they passed. He'd had a word to say about every weed and spot of peeling paint earlier in the day, so Mal'ik took that to mean he was deep in his head.

The Southern Hemisphere of Tava had been nearly leveled by the initial invasion. After the peace treaty, everything remaining had crumbled under the pressure and explosions of the militia that had fought on and eventually coalesced into the organized Resistance. Most of the humans—recent immigrants pushed out to the largely unoccupied region in an ill-considered landgrab by a Human species state bulging at its seams—abandoned it. All that remained were the humans who had lived there for generations, largely suffering from a crumbling infrastructure and pockmarked by the violent Resistance who wanted all species states out no matter the cost.

As part of the force left there after the war to stabilize

the region, Mal'ik had lived among the people of Southern Tava for nearly as long as he had lived among his own family. They didn't deserve the danger and poverty they lived with, but he hadn't been able to fix it.

So Mal'ik was not surprised that even Turner's mind might have been too full to focus on nonsense. But as they entered the courtyard in which the meeting was to take place, Turner had relaxed his shoulders, and the first words out of his mouth were to complain about sitting for an extended time outdoors in such a hot, humid, and down-right muggy climate.

Word must have gotten around about Turner's manner, because Governor Tesh just smiled and shook his hand in the human greeting.

Mal'ik wasn't pleased about a meeting outdoors either. Too many entrances and sightlines. He'd called for another guard to be present, and she stood above them on a balcony.

Mal'ik had tuned out the conversation to scan the surrounding hallways and entrances when, an hour or so into the meeting, he caught a whiff of sun-dried linens. He snapped his head back to Turner and inhaled deeply.

Yes, sun-dried linens and a tint of anxiety. Turner hadn't been exaggerating when he'd said it was humid. Sweat beaded along his hairline and dripped down his neck, carving out paths in the thick cream over his pulse points.

The governor had noticed it too and had leaned forward subtly, nostrils flaring.

Mal'ik hit his comms. "Yela, get scent-neutralizing cream and meet me in the western hallway. Now."

"Yes, sir."

Mal'ik stepped forward and grabbed Turner's upper arm. The muscles under his hand tensed, and Mal'ik smelled the startle, then a whiff of that warm, earthy scent that made him want to growl. He tightened his fingers into the human's bicep and glanced at Governor Tesh across the table. He saw the beginnings of a sly, suspicious smile.

"I need to speak with you." Mal'ik didn't wait for Turner to reply. He pulled Turner up and out of his chair, the human too startled to fight back, and dragged him away to the opening of a hallway.

Once they'd turned the corner, Turner wrenched himself free. "What the hell are you doing?"

"Your scent cream is sweating off," Mal'ik growled. "I can smell you."

Turner's eyes widened, and Mal'ik was hit with the full force of a wave of sweet, earthy, yearning promise. A shudder went down Mal'ik's spine. He turned away and took a step back.

"I don't have any more on me."

For the first time in their brief acquaintance, Turner's voice sounded small and unsure. Mal'ik fought the urge to turn back around, run his thumb over those sharp cheek-bones, and soothe him. As though Turner needed soothing and *Mal'ik* could provide it for him.

"Yela is bringing some now," he said instead. The scent faded, and Mal'ik finally glanced back at Turner to see him rubbing the remnants of the cream into more even coverage over his skin.

They stood there for a few moments, avoiding each other's eyes, Turner's fingers still fluttering along his pulse point. Then Mal'ik heard Turner inhale to speak.

"Thank you." He dropped his hand from his throat and looked up at Mal'ik with his face open and devoid of the usual hint of mockery and superiority. "I know it's your job to protect my life and not my business interests, and I appreciate that you didn't let me lose my advantage back there. I'd be hamstrung in these talks if they could smell my thinking."

Mal'ik just nodded. It *wasn't* his job to protect Turner's work. In fact, his government would probably have preferred if Mal'ik had just let Turner's olfactory mask slip. But Mal'ik found the thought of Turner's truths— sunshine, fresh air, anxiety, delicious want—slipping out past his defenses without his consent oddly unacceptable.

"Sir, I have it here." Yela arrived a moment later and held out the small container.

Turner took it with a grateful smile. "Thank you." He opened it and started liberally applying it to his throat and wrists, and the clean smell of him disappeared again. "No more meetings outside after this. Inside with good air conditioning only."

"I'll make sure of it." Mal'ik nodded to the small jar. "And keep that on you."

Turner tucked the container into his pocket with a wry twist of his lips. "I will."

OLIVER SHUT the door on the first official day of negotiations and rubbed his eyes with his thumb and forefinger. The first couple of days were always the hardest. Numerous dossiers could only get him so far, so he always had to spend those forty-eight hours or so absorbing as much information as he could about as many of the players as he could. His brain ached with the effort of synthesizing it all and strategizing his attacks.

He couldn't get it wrong this time, not again. Dominic was in an entirely different system, and yet Oliver could feel his older brother's eyes on him—just waiting for him to trip up so he could finally push Oliver out of their father's gaze altogether.

Oliver swallowed and shook his head. He couldn't think about the consequences of failure, or he'd only guarantee it.

A shower would help. And it would get off all the cream clogging his pores. Its usefulness could not be overstated, and he'd already ordered more, but the feel of it on him made his skin crawl. He didn't have the nose of a klah'eel, but even some subconscious part of his brain tripped over the fact that he couldn't smell himself.

He could smell Captain Mal'ik, though.

Oliver stripped off his clothes, stepped into the hot spray of the shower, and let his aching mind wander to where it really wanted to go. And where it wanted to go was to the big, scarred, grizzled old warrior that stood guard at his back all day and the way he smelled like pure masculinity. Oliver wouldn't mind having him at his back just a little closer.

Which was absurd because Oliver never felt that way, not anymore, not for years now. The thought of all the stickiness and fluids and *mess* involved with being intimate with someone made him shudder and not in a good way.

But if Mal'ik wanted to make a mess of him... Oliver trailed his soapy hand down to where his cock was starting to—

He tore his hand away.

No. Feeding his obsession like that would not help, and if he wasn't careful, more than his scent would give him away. The Klah'Eel officials he worked with would certainly notice if he started making doe eyes at his bodyguard.

That shifty, smarmy Governor Tesh already had his suspicions after that slipup in the courtyard.

When Mal'ik had heroically saved him and—oh look, his exhausted mind had stumbled back to its favorite topic. Oliver turned off the water before his urges could get the better of him. He had the fate of half a planet to plan, a brother to dethrone, and the love of his father to win back.

THE VERY FIRST part of Oliver's plan was education. It was a vital piece of infrastructure, but one his father would consider acceptable to compromise on. It was where he could give a little if he had to.

He stared at the summary of Southern Tava's current education system while he sat at the breakfast table but couldn't make himself see it. His attention kept wandering over his shoulder to where he could feel the bulk of Captain Mal'ik standing at the door. His awareness kept straining to catch a whiff of him, or to hear him shift position, to turn around and see him.

Oliver sighed. If that was where his focus wanted to be, he might as well use it.

He turned in his chair to look up—he always had to look up farther than expected when he finally let himself look at all—at Mal'ik. "Where did you go to school?"

Mal'ik looked away from the doorway across from him and blinked. "I didn't."

"What?" Oliver looked down at his summary. There were schools in Southern Tava, and he'd been assured that at least the region was fairly standard in this way. "What do you mean you didn't go to school?"

Mal'ik raised an eyebrow. "I mean I didn't go to school."

"But you must have been educated somewhere." Oliver turned all the way around in his chair to face him fully.

"You don't *seem* like an idiot at least, and I like to think I can spot them a mile away."

"The Gat'Raph educated me when I joined."

Oliver had heard of the Gat'Raph, the best of the best Klah'Eel warriors. He had also known Mal'ik had been one. Garin had only told him about five times. But he hadn't realized they were also a source of education. He frowned down at his summary again.

"There weren't many schools when I was young, and there were none near my village in Klah," Mal'ik continued, tilting his head a little at Oliver. "There still isn't."

That was the piece Oliver was missing. The existence of schools was all well and good, but if the distribution was uneven then they might as well not exist. "Are there plans for one?"

"I wouldn't know."

Oliver looked back up at Mal'ik and found himself looking into those intense orange eyes. "Do you wish you could have gone to school?"

Mal'ik didn't reply right away, and Oliver wondered if he'd gotten too personal. It wasn't really Oliver's business. The job description was to stay by his side, not listen to his chatter and put up with all his questions.

"I am grateful for what the Gat'Raph gave me," Mal'ik finally replied, and that wasn't exactly an answer, but Oliver managed to clamp his teeth down around a follow-up question before he spent all breakfast and then some begging for attention from a man who had a job to do.

He turned back to his work and half-eaten meal. Oliver had a job to do as well. He was no longer so convinced of his ability to compromise on education. In fact, given that capable young men were apparently being drawn into the military instead of the industry for want of education, he rather thought that the Turner business interests would require a different approach.

"YOU WANT *how much* directed toward local schools?" The finance minister gaped at Oliver. And the education minister went a little pale, as though he wasn't even sure what he would do with that money. Which was fine because Oliver would be the one directing its allocation.

"I don't know why you're taking that tone." Oliver leaned back in his seat and tapped his finger against the hardwood table. He knew exactly why the minister was taking that tone—the figure was astronomical—but he would just have to swallow it. "My family will be putting that and another fifty percent on top of it toward education in the region."

"That's as much as the education budget for the entirety of Klah," the finance minister finally managed to stammer.

"Well, frankly, I think that's absurd, but that's your problem." Oliver shrugged a single shoulder, and the finance minister's eyes nearly popped out of his skull. His cheeks started to turn purple on his dusky skin, and Oliver wished he could smell, like klah'eel. What did someone that was positively livid smell like?

He glanced at Mal'ik to see him with the ghost of a smile on the non-mangled half of his mouth. It must smell quite amusing then.

"My family will be opening numerous mining and industrial facilities in the Southern Tava hinterlands, and we have no desire for illiterate employees nor to lose high-potential young talent to better-served areas. The cities may be educated, but the number of schools near our planned locations is abysmal." Oliver cut a carefully constructed bored gaze back to the finance minister. "You understand we can't possibly make these investments knowing that we'll be building on an uneducated and potentially dwindling workforce."

The finance minister didn't reply immediately, so Oliver carried on as though he had.

"I'm glad you understand me." He leaned forward and addressed the still shell-shocked education minister. "Now that that's settled, I have some detailed plans on how I want these funds allocated, but you're welcome to give input."

The finance minister stood and sputtered something about needing to speak with the head of treasury and then left while Oliver went over plans with the education minister. Oliver was certain he'd push back on his proposed budget, but by then, Oliver would have won over the education minister, and if all went according to plan, the military minister as well. Once he had those two, he would be in an even stronger position.

It turned out that despite all his mousiness in previous interactions, the education minister did have some good ideas, and their planning went late into the evening. It was dark by the time they were done, and Oliver was hungry and thirsty and very, very pleased with himself.

He waited until he and Mal'ik were alone in an arcade and heading back to their quarters before turning to him. He smirked, practically bubbling with pride and barely able to tamp it down. "A few hours of arguments, a lot of money, and now every village in Southern Tava will have a nearby school."

Mal'ik raised his horned eyebrow, but he gave him a smile that pulled his scarred lips around one of his tusks in a way that made Oliver's insides flutter. "I didn't see any papers being signed."

Oliver waved a hand and tsked. "That part will come. For now, have someone bring dinner to my quarters and a bottle of whatever it is that's used to celebrate around here."

Mal'ik relayed the order into his earpiece as Oliver strode along the hallway, hands twitching with energy. He hadn't brought an entourage, though one had certainly been expected of him. He didn't need one, and he didn't want one. He didn't like people he didn't trust hanging around him, and he didn't trust anyone. He only tolerated bodyguards because he knew what could happen without them.

But there were times when even Oliver could think that was lonely, and now here he was riding high on success with no one to care about it.

When they got to Oliver's room, Oliver turned to face Mal'ik and lifted his chin. "Will you come in? Having a drink *with* someone is a celebration, but having a drink by myself is just pathetic, and I'm clearly not pathetic."

Mal'ik frowned. "I'm on duty," he replied in his ever-calm, even voice.

"You won't be when the night guards get here," Oliver pointed out, and then he could have kicked himself.

The man got two hours alone at most before he had to go to sleep then wake up and be glued to Oliver's demanding side all over again. Of course he didn't want to spend *that* time with Oliver too. He hadn't asked Oliver to provide schools to remote villages; Oliver had done that all on his own because he—

Oliver grimaced. Because he wanted Captain Mal'ik.

And Captain Mal'ik *knew* that. He had smelled it on him that day in the courtyard. Oliver felt a hot flush behind his ears. Mal'ik was so calm and steady, Oliver occasionally forgot that Mal'ik *knew*. Of course he wouldn't want to spend his limited free time in a room with a client practically salivating over him.

"Never mind. Of course, that's your time, forget I asked." Oliver turned back to his door, ducked his head, and fumbled with the keypad. He couldn't remember the stupid code, and he just wanted to get the stupid door open. All his previous jubilation drained away like it had never been there, spiraling down into some black abyss in the floor, and Oliver wished it would take his body with it.

"I'll come in."

Oliver's head popped up, and his heart jumped into his throat. "You will? I mean, you don't have to."

Mal'ik nodded, his scarred lips twitching into a little smile. "Once the guards get here. I'll come in."

"Wonderful." Oliver grinned. The muscles of his cheeks rebelled against the unfamiliar feeling. He forced the expression into a much more reasonable smile. "I'll see you later then."

The code came back to him, and he escaped into the room, shutting the door behind him. He leaned against it and chewed on his lip, his stomach swirling and his heart hammering.

Oliver had made better decisions in his life. He'd been heady with his success, feeling powerful and bold. And now he felt stupid. What was his plan anyway? Did he have a plan? Dinner and a drink? And then a good night, it was nice to have you over, please ignore the obvious pheromones I'm pumping into the room?

Or he could throw himself at Mal'ik like a dog in heat. That was an option. Oliver gave that maybe a fifty percent chance of success. It really depended on whether the shudder that had passed through Mal'ik's muscular body that day in the courtyard had been disgust or restraint.

Oliver scoffed and finally pushed himself off the door and headed to the bedroom. He had too much self-respect —and fear of outright rejection—to do that. But the scent-neutralizing cream was coming off. He'd never be able to relax with it and the accumulated grime of the day still sticking to his skin and his hair.

And if it meant Mal'ik knew exactly what he wanted, then so be it. It had been years and years since Oliver had wanted anyone. He had been afraid he'd never want again, so he might as well seize it now.

He took a hot shower, scrubbing himself thoroughly but in as businesslike a manner as he could. He didn't want any repeats of last night's temptation. He was just pulling on clean lounge clothes when he heard the heavy knock on the door.

He opened the door to see Mal'ik with a food-laden tray balanced on his prosthetic hand and a bottle gripped in his other. His beautiful orange eyes widened and his nostrils flared, and Oliver immediately regretted his decision to leave off the cream.

"You're not wearing your scent cream."

"No." Oliver swallowed. "I can go put some on, though, if you prefer?"

"No." Mal'ik shook his head and finally crossed the threshold. "It's fine."

Oliver peaked out at the two guards on either side of the door. Neither were facing them, but Oliver didn't know what they smelled.

He shut the door quickly, then casually crossed to the small couch and draped himself over it to watch as Mal'ik set the tray down. "So, what did you bring?"

"Nothing." Mal'ik set the tray aside and moved to Oliver's side of the table and the single couch they would share. "A servant brought this with the guards. I just carried it in."

"A surprise for us both then." Oliver didn't wait for Mal'ik to sit before grabbing one of the plates. He was starving, and while klah'eel food didn't have as many spices as human food, the meats were unbeatable.

"Actually, this I did bring." Mal'ik set the bottle he was still holding on the table. Oliver thought he might have detected a hint of nerves in the way Mal'ik played his calloused fingers over its neck before letting it go. "I thought you might like it."

"Really?" Oliver set his plate aside to grab the bottle, a little bloom of warmth going off in his chest. Its label was written in Klah'Eel, and it was paper, so it didn't do him the courtesy of rearranging into legible Universal like a data tablet would have. He looked up at Mal'ik with a smile. "And what about it do you think I'd like?"

"It's astringency."

Oliver barked out a laugh that surprised even him. "Are you trying to say something about my personality, Mal'ik?"

"Nothing you don't already know, I'm sure." Mal'ik gave him a smile that pulled at his scars and at Oliver's heartstrings.

Being called astringent should not feel like a compliment, but Oliver grabbed a glass and opened the bottle, feeling oddly warm and seen.

Mal'ik nudged his plate back toward him. "You might want to put more food in your stomach before you break into that."

"I just want a taste."

As soon as the first sip hit the back of Oliver's throat,

he could see why Mal'ik had warned him to eat first. He swallowed and blew hard out his nose, eyes watering.

"Burns a lot and hard to swallow." He blinked rapidly and wiped the moisture from his eyes. "You're right. It does remind me of me."

That earned him a deep, booming laugh from Mal'ik, and something went gooey and self-satisfied in Oliver's chest. He settled into the couch, holding his plate of food, and watched Mal'ik serve himself. He had such big, careful hands—mechanical and skin—and he moved so slowly and methodically. He was calming just to watch.

Oliver's cheeks suddenly went warm as he realized they'd been sitting in silence for almost a minute as he trailed his eyes up Mal'ik's muscular forearm. He yanked his gaze back to Mal'ik's scarred face and grasped around for a conversational thread. "So, why did you leave the Gat'Raph?"

Mal'ik raised an eyebrow at Oliver as he spooned a green sauce over a dumpling, as though the answer were obvious. "I was retired out."

Oliver blushed, and his eyes flicked down to the mechanical arm Mal'ik used so deftly. "Oh. Because of your injury?"

Mal'ik chuckled. "No, that happened years ago, and I served for many more after it. But the Gat'Raph retires all of their soldiers once we reach a certain age. They need to keep their resources focused."

Oliver sat up. "So they throw you out like trash?"

Mal'ik tilted his head, those orange eyes warm, and replied after a moment. "No. We usually retire into the Klah'Eel's armed forces. The government gets highly trained soldiers, and the Gat'Raph both curries favor and keeps their forces lean. It is a good deal."

"Was it a good deal for you?"

"Yes." Mal'ik took a sip of the astringent liquor he'd brought as though it were nothing, and Oliver let himself be distracted for just a moment by the movement of his throat. "I actually requested to retire a year early."

Oliver flicked his eyes back up to Mal'ik's face, and he could tell by the twitch of his lips around his tusk that he'd been caught staring. "Why did you do that?"

"Because the Gat'Raph was pulling out of Southern Tava, and I wanted to stay."

That chased out the thoughts of Oliver's tongue running up the column of Mal'ik's throat. Oliver set his plate down in his lap and turned to face him more fully. "Why?"

Mal'ik's small smile spread to a larger, almost bashful one, and he shook his head. "You have a lot of questions." But he continued before Oliver had to reply. "The people still needed me. I didn't want to abandon them."

Somehow that answer didn't surprise Oliver. He didn't know this Captain Mal'ik, but Oliver could tell he was the type to give of himself for others. What a foreign concept. Oliver looked away, took a sip of that burning liquor, and tried not to flinch. He didn't think he'd ever cared about anyone enough to... Well, he didn't know if he'd ever cared about anyone at all.

He cared deeply about his father's *opinion*, but that wasn't quite the same. And perhaps as a child, he had cared about his brother, but the foolishness of that had been driven home quite quickly in the Turner household. His mother? But he didn't even remember her; she left them before his brain was capable of forming long-term memories. He knew of her only from the tabloids and upper crust gossip.

"I think you'll help them."

"What?" Oliver's head popped up and yanked his

thoughts away from his dismal family. He found himself caught in Mal'ik's thoughtful gaze, and his heart skipped. He licked his lips.

"The things you say in the meetings you go to. About systems, and infrastructure, and investment." Mal'ik leaned forward. "Do you mean them?"

Strangely, Oliver had to bite his tongue to hold back a denial. Mal'ik was looking at him with too much intensity and too much…hope? Oliver's first instinct was to crush that hope because surely it was misplaced, but he made himself sit still and answer honestly.

He nodded. "Yes. I believe the region has a lot of potential. I believe it's plagued by incompetence and corruption, and"—he shrugged—"I believe I can do better. I'm good at improving things."

Mal'ik smiled at him in a way that made Oliver's heart race.

The words were out of Oliver's mouth before he could stop them. "It doesn't mean that I care." He swallowed. Those warm eyes on him felt too good. Better to rip off the Band-Aid and set the record straight now. "I came here to do a job. That's what I care about."

"Alright." Mal'ik nodded, but his eyes didn't harden in the way Oliver had expected. They stayed soft and warm. He put another dumpling into his mouth, as though Oliver's clarification didn't bother him at all.

So, Oliver followed his lead and turned his attention to the succulent cubes of meat he'd decided were his favorite. His heart rate slowed to a normal level, and after a few moments, he felt comfortable sneaking glances at his companion again.

Captain Mal'ik was clearly strong and capable; he was definitely old enough to have been in the original invasion of Southern Tava. And judging from his words earlier, he had been part of the occupying force for years afterward.

"Do you have any advice?"

Mal'ik froze. Then his brows furrowed as he finished chewing and swallowed. "What?"

"Advice," Oliver repeated. "Concerns, thoughts, opinions, etcetera. On Southern Tava."

Mal'ik frowned. "Me?"

Oliver frowned back and squinted at him. "Yes, of course. You were there for years, right? You chose to stay there. You clearly care."

"Very much."

"So, what are your thoughts?"

"I—" Mal'ik looked away, his frown deepening.

Oliver cocked his head in bafflement. Surely the man had thoughts, especially on something he cared about. Oliver had thoughts on everything, including things he *didn't* care about.

Finally, Mal'ik shook his head. "It's never been my place to have any thoughts on the matter. I do my duty. I do my job. It's people like you that have thoughts on things."

"That's silly." Once again, Oliver's mouth ran away with his thoughts before he could stop it, and his hand gesticulated wildly. "You have years of experience, probably decades. You've had a closer look at the problems than any of us, and you're not an idiot. Why the hell shouldn't it be your place to have thoughts?"

Mal'ik gaped at him, and Oliver flushed.

"Sorry." He dropped his hands. "I shouldn't push."

"No, it's fine." Mal'ik inhaled deeply and sat up straighter. His brows furrowed again, but he spoke. "I think the Klah'Eel forget the region's history and underestimate the effect that history has on the people."

"The history as in the invasion?"

"Before that." Mal'ik leaned forward again and put his elbows on his knees. His shoulders loosened, as though now that he was speaking it wasn't so difficult to keep going. "For generations before the invasion, Southern Tava was part of the Human species state in name only. The Humans basically ignored them, and they were independent for all intents and purposes. And they liked it that way."

Oliver nodded, his history coming back to him now. He had dismissed it as well, thinking it couldn't matter anymore after all that happened. "But then we started dealing with overpopulation, and we started settling more people into the region."

"To bolster your claim on it against the Klah'Eel." Mal'ik gave him a half smile that Oliver returned.

"Allegedly." Oliver chuckled. Officially the Human government denied that accusation, and the two sides had agreed to disagree on the subject at the signing of the peace treaty.

"In any case," Mal'ik shrugged, "more humans came, more Human species state oversight came, then the Klah'Eel invasion came, most of the new humans left, and here we are."

"Meaning the people the Klah'Eel are trying to rule are the people that never wanted to be ruled by a species state in the first place." Oliver chuckled to himself and leaned back into the couch.

"Precisely." Mal'ik took another gulp of liquor and sighed.

Oliver grinned at him. "See. You *do* have useful thoughts."

Mal'ik glanced at him and then looked away again quickly. "If you say so."

"I do."

Mal'ik's scarred lips twitched in that little smile Oliver was so drawn to and didn't reply.

They lapsed into silence.

Mal'ik sat with his elbows on his knees, twirling his mostly empty cup of liquor in his hands. Oliver sat next to him, fighting and failing to keep his eyes off him.

He was breathtaking. Oliver literally felt his breathing constrict when he looked at him, and he didn't rightly know why. Klah'Eel were not attractive by human standards—tusks, sharp teeth, heavy brows—and Mal'ik had scars twisting over his face and a missing arm to boot. But those were the things Oliver felt himself most drawn to.

Mal'ik had survived. He was strong. And while people like Oliver and everyone he had ever known talked in circles and gave orders and called it power, Mal'ik embodied power in a way that felt real. And he used it to protect, to care, to stand guard.

Oliver licked his lips and met Mal'ik's orange eyes. The big man had gone still, his face serious, and his gaze bore into Oliver.

Suddenly, Mal'ik set his cup on the table, clapped his hands onto his own muscular thighs, and pushed himself to stand. "I should go."

Oliver's heart clenched as his window of opportunity threatened to slam closed. He knew he should let Mal'ik leave. He shouldn't embarrass himself or expose this weakness, or indulge this distraction, but the man was about to slip through Oliver's fingers, and it made him want to cry.

"Will you fuck me?"

Chapter Three

OLIVER ALMOST GASPED, and he bit hard on his bottom lip to keep himself from saying more. Justifications beat against the back of his teeth, as though *will you fuck me* wasn't enough and he needed to make his case as to why Mal'ik's answer should be yes.

God, Oliver hoped his answer would be yes.

Slowly, Mal'ik turned to face Oliver, looking down at him on the couch from his towering height. "Do you want me to fuck you?"

That startled a laugh out of Oliver. "Do I want you to? How can you ask that? I must smell like a bitch in heat to you."

"You don't. You smell…" Mal'ik paused, and his eyes narrowed as he seemed to search for the right word. "… like molasses."

"Like molasses?" Oliver wrinkled his nose and looked down at the couch. "You know, I think I preferred the dog. No one likes molasses."

"I do."

Oliver's breath caught at the certainty in Mal'ik's tone,

and Oliver's eyes flickered back up to his face. Mal'ik's expression didn't say anything. Oliver wondered if his smell did. This would be so much easier if he could smell the arousal on Mal'ik as easily as Mal'ik could smell it on him. Assuming there was anything to smell on the bigger man or if anyone could even make it out over Oliver's cloud of pheromones.

Oliver shifted in his seat. "So then, is that a yes?"

He tensed as Mal'ik took a step forward and leaned over him. The big man grabbed the couch on either side of him, bracketing him in and leaning close until, for a brief, exciting second, Oliver was sure he was going to kiss him. Then he stopped, close enough for Oliver to feel the heat of him all around him and to smell the musk of him that even Oliver could make out.

"You didn't answer my question." Mal'ik's voice rumbled down Oliver's spine. "Do you want me to fuck you, Oliver?"

Oliver's stomach swooped at the sound of his name in Mal'ik's voice. His fingers twitched with the desire to twist the front of Mal'ik's shirt and pull him closer, but he didn't know if he was allowed.

"Very much," he breathed.

"Then yes." Mal'ik crushed their lips together almost violently.

Oliver gasped, and Mal'ik swept his tongue inside his mouth and kissed him deeply. Mal'ik pressed him back into the couch, and Oliver let him, let him push him and manhandle him and trap him against the soft cushions and fabric.

Mal'ik left off kissing him to scrape his tusk up Oliver's jaw and worry at his ear, and Oliver squirmed and whimpered as though the shell of his ear had a hotline straight to his cock. He grabbed Mal'ik's shoulders and dug his fingers into the muscles he'd barely been able to keep his eyes off.

"Yes, I will fuck you, Oliver Turner," Mal'ik growled into his ear, and without warning, he grabbed Oliver's legs and hooked them around his hips. He wrapped his arms around him and lifted him into the air.

Oliver yelped and clung to Mal'ik's neck as Mal'ik carried him into the bedroom. The show of strength sent a thrill down his spine, and he pressed his cock into the hard ripples of Mal'ik's abs and groaned.

"Oh fuck." Oliver nuzzled into the hollow behind Mal'ik's ear and rocked his hips against his body. Mal'ik dropped his hands to Oliver's ass and dug his fingers into the muscle as Oliver pushed against him.

"That feel good to you?" Mal'ik nipped Oliver's ear. Oliver's back hit the wall as Mal'ik pushed him up against it. It gave him more leverage to rut against him, and Oliver whined and increased his pace.

"Yes."

"Maybe I'll make you finish like this." Mal'ik used his grip on Oliver's ass to roll his hips against him, controlling his movements and rubbing Oliver's cock against him.

Oliver whined again and shook his head. "No." But the sharpness of his tone was ruined by breathiness as a wave of pleasure rolled through him. He screwed up his face and pressed his forehead against Mal'ik's to look into his beautiful, intense eyes. "No, that's not what you said."

"No, it's not," Mal'ik agreed. He tightened his grip on Oliver to pull him away from the wall and then turned and dumped him on the bed.

Oliver's stomach dropped out as he fell, but before he had the time to panic, his back hit the soft comforter and he was looking up at Mal'ik. Mal'ik stood between his spread legs and smirked down at him. "I said I'd fuck you, but I didn't say how many other things I was going to do to you first."

"Is that a promise?" Oliver shot back, and he arched his back in a way he knew would make him look good.

But Mal'ik's dirty smirk went soft, and he put his hand on Oliver's knee in a way that felt more intimate than sensuous. "Everything I say to you is a promise, Oliver," he said in a low voice that vibrated through Oliver's chest, making it tighten.

Oliver's lips parted as he stared up into Mal'ik's intense eyes, feeling very exposed even though he was still fully dressed.

Mal'ik rubbed his thumb over the inside of Oliver's knee.

Oliver didn't know what to say to that, and he felt an immense amount of relief when the serious earnestness in Mal'ik's eyes gave way to leering intent.

"Now take off your clothes," Mal'ik ordered.

Oliver scrambled to comply, yanking off his shirt, clumsy with anticipation. It got caught around his shoulders, and he had to twist it a few times to get it over his head. By the time he'd freed himself from the fabric, Mal'ik was stepping out of his own pants.

Oliver stared at him, gaping slightly with his mouth watering.

"God, you look good," Oliver managed. His eyes roved down that expanse of dusky, green-tinged skin. Mal'ik's huge shoulders with a scratched-up leather harness holding on his metal arm. His broad, musclebound chest with scars streaking down one side, his chiseled abs, the pronounced V of his hips, down to the jut of his already hard, girthy cock. Oliver had never wanted to give head before in his life, but all of a sudden, he was dying to know what that would feel like in his mouth.

"You're not naked," Mal'ik growled, and Oliver dragged his gaze back up to Mal'ik's face.

Mal'ik looked like something out of the wet dreams Oliver never had, and he wasn't totally convinced he wasn't asleep now. Then Mal'ik's words caught up with him, and he hurriedly started undoing his pants.

As soon as he'd undone the buttons, Mal'ik's big hands batted Oliver's away and yanked his pants and underwear down in one motion, leaving Oliver bare and stretched out on the bed before him.

Oliver bit his lip and cocked an eyebrow. "Better?"

Mal'ik huffed a laugh. "Almost."

Then Mal'ik grabbed Oliver's hips, and Oliver let out a surprised yelp as Mal'ik flipped him onto his stomach. Then Mal'ik yanked him back and pulled his ass up into the air, with his knees braced under him. Oliver's balls tightened as a surprising shudder of arousal went through him.

"What are you doing?" Oliver demanded, as though having his chest pressed into the mattress and his thighs spread wide wasn't making him drip onto the comforter below. He squirmed, confused by his own reaction.

Mal'ik pressed a kiss to the very base of Oliver's spine, right above the cleft of his ass. "I think you know."

And suddenly Oliver did know, and it hit him like a bolt of lightning and punched the air out of his chest. Twin jolts of fear and desire shot through him. No one had ever done that to him. He had never even *thought* of anyone doing that to him.

"No-no-no, Mal'ik, you don't—oh!" Oliver cut off with a gasp and jerk as Mal'ik licked along his cleft, just above his hole. Mal'ik spread Oliver with his thumbs—one soft skin, the other hard metal—and Oliver's breath came in heaving gasps. He fisted his hands in the comforter. "I don't—you don't—please—"

Oliver's words dissolved into a whimper when Mal'ik swirled his tongue over his entrance. His nerve endings lit up, and his breath hiccuped out of him as Mal'ik did it again, firm and insistent. It felt so much better than anything like that should ever feel.

"Oh fuck," he whined, and Mal'ik dragged his hips back and buried his face into Oliver's center, licking and sucking and kissing. Fuck, it felt so good; it was fucking mind-blowing. Oliver's hips twitched of their own accord, little abortive thrusts that bounced his hanging cock around in the air.

Mal'ik laughed lowly, and the vibrations sent a shock of pleasure up Oliver's spine. Then Mal'ik dug his thumbs in deeper, spread Oliver wider, and speared his tongue into Oliver's tight pucker. Oliver yowled. He dragged at the bed below him, his fists tangling in sheets. God, that was filthy. Filthy and hot and pulling a continuous string of pleasured whines and moans out of Oliver's throat.

Mal'ik's tongue was up Oliver's ass. His brain circled around the thought, over and over. Mal'ik's tongue was up Oliver's ass, and he was pretty sure he was going to come from that alone.

"Fuck, Mal'ik, I can't, I can't," he babbled as his balls drew up tight to the base of his cock.

He wasn't going to come. He couldn't possibly come. But the pleasure tightened his lower back almost painfully, and he was on some sort of edge, making him nervous and anxious. The feel of Mal'ik's tongue thrusting at his entrance overtook his mind.

Mal'ik pulled away, gave one last broad lick up Oliver's taint and over his quivering hole, and then flipped him onto his back.

Oliver let out a shuddery, relieved sob and dragged the heels of his palm over his face as the edge of his impending orgasm retreated. He felt Mal'ik's tusks against his inner thigh and looked down to see Mal'ik on his knees at the foot of his bed, nuzzling him.

"I knew you'd be fussy in bed," Mal'ik said against the sensitive skin of Oliver's inner thigh and then pressed a gentle kiss to it.

Oliver's breath hitched at the incongruous soft feel of the kiss, with the electrifying vision of Mal'ik's scarred face between his thighs, so close to his dripping cock.

"So you thought about it?" Oliver licked his lips. "What I'd be like in bed?"

Mal'ik bared his teeth and then buried his nose into the crease of Oliver's hips, his tusk brushing against Oliver's sac, making Oliver jerk. "I had to." Mal'ik tightened his grip on Oliver's thigh and inhaled deeply. "With you smelling like this, I couldn't *not* think about what you'd be like."

Oliver flushed and wondered just how strongly he was pumping his desire out into the air. But if it got him this—spread out in bed with Mal'ik between his legs, nuzzling at the base of his cock—he couldn't be sorry.

Oliver sucked in a breath when the rough pad of Mal'ik's finger rubbed over his entrance.

"Where's your lube?" Mal'ik asked, pressing and circling slowly. Not pressing inside, just teasing him.

Oliver bit his lip as his flush deepened, realizing his oversight. "I don't have any," he admitted.

Mal'ik frowned and then got up from his knees, his joints creaking. He crawled over Oliver's body, bracketing him into the bed, and looked down into his face with his too-shrewd orange eyes.

"You don't have any?" he repeated.

"No, I don't. I don't normally—that is, I never—" Oliver scowled up at Mal'ik, frustrated to be falling over his own words. "I never have occasion to use it."

Mal'ik trailed one hand down the center of Oliver's chest and caressed his fingers lightly up Oliver's cock. It was the first real touch it had gotten, and it twitched in response.

"Not even on yourself?"

That was too far. "I asked you to fuck me, not analyze my sex life," Oliver snapped.

He felt bad when Mal'ik's eyes shuttered slightly but didn't take it back. He didn't want to tell Mal'ik that he hadn't been with anyone in years. That he hadn't wanted to ever since that day. That even the thought of his own hand—the slick lube, the clinging sweat, the sticky spend—made his gorge rise.

He just wanted Mal'ik, and he didn't want to think about why or what was different with him or any of it.

But fuck, maybe he'd just ruined that too. He reached up and grabbed Mal'ik's metal wrist where it was braced on the bed beside his ear, certain the klah'eel was about to pull away.

"Mal'ik—"

But then Mal'ik kissed him, gentle and soft, and Oliver shuddered with relief.

Oliver traced his hands up Mal'ik's arms, one cool and metallic, the other warm and corded with muscle, to wrap his arms around Mal'ik's neck.

Mal'ik let out a hum of pleasure and opened Oliver's lips with his to kiss him deeper.

Oliver shivered at the taste of Mal'ik's mouth, remembering where the tongue sliding against his now had been just moments ago.

Mal'ik broke the kiss to trail his lips to Oliver's ear. "I'm not fucking you dry, Oliver."

Oliver's fingers spasmed as they dug into the meat of Mal'ik's shoulders, tightening his grip on him before he could pull away.

"I want it," he said firmly. He hadn't wanted to be fucked in years; he wasn't going to let it get away from him now.

"What else do you have?" Mal'ik asked. He petted his soft hand over Oliver's hips and smoothed his thumb over Oliver's hipbone.

Oliver relaxed when he realized Mal'ik wasn't pulling away. In fact, he was nibbling at Oliver's ear in an extremely distracting way that also seemed to indicate he was still interested. Oliver racked his brain, trying to think of anything else he had on hand that could work. It didn't take long.

"Oil." He pushed on Mal'ik's shoulders, desperate to get it now that he'd thought of it. "I have oil in the bathroom."

"I'll get it." Mal'ik pressed a firm hand into the center of Oliver's chest as he sat back on his knees.

Oliver looked down his muscular body to see Mal'ik's cock was still hard, and he almost sagged with relief. He hadn't ruined everything. Mal'ik still wanted him. Still wanted him plenty, judging by the look in his eyes as he dragged a hand from the center of Oliver's chest down his stomach to his own leaking length. He skipped Oliver's cock, though, and palmed Oliver's balls in his big hand, teasing over Oliver's taint with the pad of his middle finger, making Oliver gasp. "I want you to stay just like this and think about what I'm going to do to you."

Oliver's cock jerked, and Mal'ik chuckled lowly as he stood from the bed and walked to the bathroom. Oliver found enough breath to shout after him, "Promises, promises."

But he was too distracted by the flexing of muscle over Mal'ik's bare ass to say more. No real-life man should be able to look that good. His body reminded Oliver of the marble statues in the gardens of his family's estate. He suddenly wondered what it would feel like to lick at Mal'ik where Mal'ik had licked at him, what it would feel like to drag his own tongue over Mal'ik's hole.

He heard Mal'ik open some drawers before he came back out, holding the bottle and looking at it with a little furrow between his heavy brows.

"Is this why your skin is so soft?" he asked.

Oliver felt absurdly pleased that Mal'ik found his skin soft. Why wouldn't he? It was objectively soft because Oliver spent obscene amounts of money on things like that to make sure of it.

"Yes." Oliver braced his foot against the bed and tilted his hips. "But I can think of some better uses for it."

Mal'ik huffed a laugh, but his eyes burned into Oliver. "Can you?"

Oliver didn't reply, his throat closing with anticipation as Mal'ik advanced on him. He let out a choked sound when Mal'ik dropped to his knees at the foot of the bed and grabbed Oliver's ankle. Mal'ik pulled it out from under him so that he lay flat on the bed again, his hips at the edge of the bed and his legs dangling off it.

"You smell so fucking good." Mal'ik buried his nose back into the crease of Oliver's hips, and Oliver pushed onto his forearms to watch. Mal'ik opened his eyes and met Oliver's, and Oliver had a moment for his heart to leap in excitement before Mal'ik licked a long stripe up the length of Oliver's cock and swallowed him down.

"Oh fuck, yes." Oliver dropped his head back and let

his pleasure hiss out of him. It felt so unabashedly good. He couldn't remember the last time he had felt such a pure pleasure. Mal'ik's mouth was hot and wet, and his suction was just enough to keep all the threads of Oliver's control just out of reach. "Mal'ik, fuck, that feels good."

Then the slick pad of an oiled finger pressed against Oliver's pucker, and he stiffened. Mal'ik didn't push in, though, just rubbed and teased until Oliver's nerve endings were on fire and he was gritting his teeth so hard he thought they might crack.

"Get on with it," he ordered, opening his eyes again to glare down at Mal'ik.

Mal'ik pulled his mouth off him with a pop and a chuckle. "Fussy."

And then he pushed his finger into Oliver, up to the knuckle. Oliver arched off the bed and just managed to keep his pained cry locked behind his teeth. Oh, it had been a long time; it had been a very long time, and Oliver had never been very good at this. What the hell had he been thinking, asking a klah'eel to fuck him as though he could possibly take anything the size of Mal'ik's cock? Oh hell, he was an idiot.

"You're okay, Oliver." Mal'ik's deep rumbling voice vibrated through him, and he managed to crack his eyes back open. "You're okay. Relax for me, Oliver. Relax."

Mal'ik kept his finger buried inside him, but he stroked his metal hand over Oliver's stomach and side. He dipped his head and kissed the inside of Oliver's knee as he petted him and murmured to him.

"You're okay. Relax."

Oliver's muscles were clenching furiously around the intrusion, but Oliver forced his breaths to even out. In through his nose, out through his mouth. Focus on the feel of Mal'ik's hand and voice. In breath, out breath. His muscles started to relax and adjust.

He let out a deep sigh when the pain faded, replaced by an erotic feeling of invasion. He twitched his hips so he could feel the finger inside him and made a tiny gasp at the spark of pleasure.

"There you go," Mal'ik murmured, and he slowly started to drag the finger out. He only got it halfway out before he pushed it back in.

"Oh, that's—oh." Oliver tossed his head to the side as the sensations built. Oh, it did feel good to be penetrated like that. To feel something breaching him and pushing inside him. He opened his eyes to meet Mal'ik's orange ones and licked his lips. To feel *Mal'ik* pushing inside him.

He wondered if something showed in his eyes or in his scent because Mal'ik growled lowly and pushed in just a little faster on the next thrust.

"Oh!" Oliver shouted when Mal'ik swallowed his cock down. For a terrifying second, Oliver thought he was going to come. He twisted his fingers into the fabric of the blanket and breathed sharply, just barely managing to cling to his control as waves of pleasure washed over him. "Oh, god, Mal'ik."

Oliver kept up his litany of cursing and moaning and Mal'ik's name as Mal'ik sucked his cock and fingered him. The combination of the slight burn of intrusion with the sweet pleasure of Mal'ik's mouth was so much better than either individually. Oliver rolled his head back and forth, not caring how he looked, too caught up in the feel of it all.

He managed to nod his head furiously when Mal'ik pressed a second finger against his rim. "Yes, yes, definitely." He lifted his hips to make his point, and Mal'ik didn't make him wait. Oliver hissed a little, but the bliss coursing through his veins kept him too relaxed to care.

After just a few minutes of two fingers, Oliver pinched his brows and managed to force himself back up onto his forearms.

"Mal'ik," he panted. "I'm not—" He cut off with groan when Mal'ik circled the crown of his head with his tongue. "Fuck. I'm not going to last. Get on with it."

Mal'ik lifted off Oliver's cock with one last, long lick and then nuzzled the base of it. "You need one more."

"I don't. I don't," Oliver insisted. His cock was aching, and his balls were pulled up so tight they hurt. "I need— oh, god, fuck."

He dropped his chin to his chest when Mal'ik shoved a third finger inside him. He let out a long breath and focused on the feel of Mal'ik metal thumb smoothing over his hipbone. When Mal'ik spread his fingers, stretching Oliver's rim with intent, Oliver dropped back onto his back with a shuddery exhale and scrubbed his palms over his face.

Soon, even the discomfort of that faded, and Oliver's desperation and urgency roared back. "Mal'ik," he cried. "Please, for the love of god, I want it."

Mal'ik pulled his fingers all the way free, leaving Oliver empty, and Oliver almost screamed, but then Mal'ik stood, and Oliver's mouth went dry instead.

"Get up higher on the bed," Mal'ik ordered. He poured a generous amount of Oliver's expensive oil into his huge palm, and Oliver watched, open-mouthed, as Mal'ik wrapped his hand around his own cock, dark and flushed with blood. He pumped it a few times and grunted. "Oliver."

Oliver rushed to comply, dragging himself higher onto

the bed until his head was on the pillows. Mal'ik climbed onto the bed after him, and Oliver watched him, heart pounding with anticipation. He braced his feet on the mattress to bend his knees and let his thighs fall wide. Satisfaction thrilled through him when Mal'ik closed his eyes and shuddered.

Suddenly, Mal'ik looped his arms under Oliver's knees and lifted his hips off the bed. Oliver yelped as his weight tipped back into his shoulders and his hands scrambled for purchase before finding it against the headboard. "What the hell are you doing?"

The scars on the right side of Mal'ik's face pulled as Mal'ik smiled crookedly down at him. "Fucking you."

Oliver's breath hitched when Mal'ik settled Oliver's legs over his broad shoulders. It was a shockingly vulnerable position. More vulnerable than just having Mal'ik on top of or behind him as he'd imagined the few times he'd let his fantasies get that detailed. But he suddenly lost the ability to care when Mal'ik grabbed his hips and nudged Oliver's hole with his cockhead.

Oh god, he was finally going to have Mal'ik inside of him. His heart raced, and his breath came short and quick, as though he'd been pining for this for years rather than the days it had actually been.

Oliver opened his mouth to boss Mal'ik again but couldn't. He didn't have any words as he stared up his own body into Mal'ik's bright orange eyes. Mal'ik held his gaze, and Oliver made a choked sound as Mal'ik pushed into him slow and steady. His instincts wanted to toss his head and screw his eyes shut at the feel of being filled, but he couldn't look away. He didn't want to look away. His lower lip trembled, and a sound that should have been a moan came out more like a sob.

Mal'ik stroked Oliver's thigh with his soft hand as he

finally sheathed himself inside Oliver. "You're so fucking beautiful, Oliver."

For once, Oliver couldn't think of what to say. He was too caught up in the look in Mal'ik's eyes, the roughness of his voice, and the absolutely, utterly, and completely overwhelming feeling of being so full.

But Mal'ik saved him from that too by pulling out and then snapping back in.

"Fuck!" Oliver did throw his head back now, the word punched out of him by the shock of Mal'ik's thrust. But Mal'ik didn't give him time to catch his breath. He pounded into him, dragging out and thrusting back in before Oliver even had a chance to register the feel of that exquisite drag against his rim.

It was perfect.

It was so fucking perfect.

He writhed and twisted, but with his legs slung over Mal'ik's shoulders, Oliver didn't have any leverage, so all he could do was take it and twist his fingers into his hair and babble.

He couldn't stop the words from spilling out of his mouth; he couldn't even decide what they would be before they were already flowing out of him. "Yes, yes, fuck yes, Mal'ik." He pulled at his hair and moaned. "God, that's amazing. Oh fuck."

He opened his eyes to stare up his own clenching stomach to Mal'ik's snarling face above him. His cock bounced between them, an almost angry red now. Mal'ik adjusted his grip and hit a spot inside Oliver that felt painfully good, and his cock kicked and drooled precum over his belly.

"I want to come." Oliver licked his lips. "Mal'ik, fuck, please, I want to come."

"Yeah?" Mal'ik dug his fingers into Oliver's hips. "You want to come all over yourself, Oliver?"

A jolt of electricity shot down Oliver's spine. "*Yes.*"

He thought of his own thick spend shooting from his cock and onto his chest and neck, and instead of instinctual panicked disgust, he felt a desperate need.

"Yes, fuck, I want that, Mal'ik," he whined. "I want to come on myself."

"Do it," Mal'ik ordered, his voice impossibly low. "Do it, Oliver. Make yourself come."

Oliver's hand shot up between his legs and grabbed hold of his sticky cock. He didn't have any of the oil Mal'ik had used and his grip was rough and full of friction, but he couldn't be bothered if it hurt.

He jacked himself frantically, mewling and sobbing at the feel of his own hand on his cock and Mal'ik pistoning inside him. He wasn't going to last long; he wasn't going to last any time at all. He was going to completely come apart. He was going to shatter.

A cry tore from his throat as he finally burst into pieces. His cock kicked and pulsed and shot cum straight up to his face. He felt a hot splatter against his chin and then his throat, and he moaned. The mess of his spend slicked his grip, and he kept milking his cock as aftershocks of pleasure shuddered through him, sparked again and again by the feel of Mal'ik thrusting into him.

"Oliver." Mal'ik's grip on his hips became bruising, and he sped up his thrusts even faster. "Oliver, I'm going to come."

"On me," Oliver found himself demanding, and as soon as the words left his mouth, it suddenly became vitally important. "Come on me, Mal'ik. Please, please, I want it on me."

"Oh fuck, Oliver."

Mal'ik pulled out and dropped over him, bending Oliver near in half. He grabbed his own cock and stroked once, twice, and then was coming with a shout. Oliver moaned again as Mal'ik pumped his cum onto him, painting his chest and his stomach with rope after rope of white. It was filthy and hot and sticky, and Oliver shuddered as a profound mix of relief and pleasure shivered through him.

After what felt like ages and gallons, Mal'ik let out a heaving sigh and finally dropped his hand from his length and down onto the bed beside Oliver. He dropped his forehead onto Oliver's shoulder and panted, and Oliver reached up to run his fingers through his dark hair as he gulped deep breaths of his own.

He was still floating. Weightless and happy and sated. He didn't think he'd ever felt this peaceful in his life. Mal'ik made a pleased hum and pressed his lips to the underside of Oliver's jaw.

Then he finally pushed off Oliver and fell onto his back beside him. Oliver winced as he stretched his legs straight out again, muscles protesting as they unbent from their contortions.

The movement caused the puddles of cum on him to ripple, and one overflowed out of the divot of his hip and dripped down his side. He looked down at himself and started crashing back out of whatever fucked out headspace he'd been in.

What the hell had he just done?

His breath started to speed up again, quick and sharp.

What sort of fucking fool had he just made of himself? He had just writhed on his bed with a cock up his ass, *begging* to be come on. He had literally begged to come all over himself and then begged for Mal'ik's spend all over him too. How the fuck was he supposed to live that down?

"Oliver." Mal'ik started to reach for him, and Oliver sat up abruptly.

The congealing semen dripped over his collarbone and down his chest, and he gagged. He swung his legs out of the bed and strode to the bathroom, fighting not to run for it.

"Oliver!"

He stepped into the shower and turned on the head to full power. The water here wasn't instantly hot like on his ship, and it hit him with an icy blast that took his breath away, but he didn't care. He just wanted to be clean; he just needed everything off him now.

"Oliver, are you alright?" Oliver could see the dark bulk of Mal'ik standing in the doorway through the translucent shower curtain. His voice was deep and even, but Oliver heard a thread of urgency and he cringed.

Now that the panic of being dirty had been assuaged by the water sluicing everything off his skin, he had even more emotional room for shame and embarrassment. He didn't want to look at Mal'ik after the way he'd just behaved, and he turned away to lean his head back into the stream of water. He swallowed to make sure his voice would come out steady.

"Yes, I'm fine," he said. "Thank you. That was perfect."

Thank you. That was perfect. Oliver winced and bit his tongue before it could say something else equally stupid. Who said that after sex?

Mal'ik didn't respond right away, and Oliver scrubbed his hair and chewed on his lip as he tried to figure out what to do. He should probably at least look at the man. Invite him into the shower so he could clean off as well? The water was warm now.

But he couldn't make his hand reach for the edge of

the shower curtain. He was paralyzed. He was too afraid of what he'd see when he looked at Mal'ik—judgment, disgust, concern, pity?—and too afraid of what Mal'ik might see when he looked at him because he felt raw and flayed. And he was too embarrassed by how he'd behaved to face it.

After a long moment, Mal'ik's form twisted as he turned away from the door. "Good night, Oliver."

"Yes, good night. Sleep well," Oliver called back and promptly wanted to bash his head through the tile wall. Was everything he said going to be the absolute worst possible option?

He heard Mal'ik's heavy footfalls walk away from the bathroom, but then any other sounds he might have been making were covered by the patter of the shower. So Oliver stayed in the stall, letting the hot water race over his skin, even once it had heated to the point of discomfort and then slight pain. He waited until he was sure Mal'ik was gone and then waited some more until he had managed to gather up the courage to come out of his hiding place and back into the bedroom.

Chapter Four

THE NEXT MORNING, Mal'ik paused before opening his door into the hallway.

He wasn't hesitating.

He was pausing to give himself more time to gather his wits. To steel himself. The guards standing across the hall in front of Oliver's door wouldn't be the same guards he'd had to walk past last night, still smelling of sex and Oliver. But they would have heard about his walk of shame. He hadn't sworn his guards to secrecy. He hadn't said anything other than good night and to wake him if anything happened, even though there could have been no doubt in their minds what he'd just done.

He exhaled heavily. What had he just done?

To sleep with an assignment—no, to have sex with an assignment; Oliver clearly hadn't wanted him to stay beyond that—was beyond unprofessional and beyond fool-ish. He would have never thought himself capable.

But no klah'eel would be able to blame him, not really. A man like Oliver, smelling the way he did, looking at Mal'ik the way he had, *asking* him—him, of all people—to fuck him. Mal'ik shuddered. He'd have never been able to say no to that.

And he hadn't.

And now, here he was, *pausing* behind his door because he didn't want to deal with the consequences of his actions. Unacceptable.

He pushed the door open and stepped out into the hall. The two second-shift night guards looked up at him and, to their credit, had no reaction other than to nod.

"Good morning, sir," said the tall human on the left. "Our shift was quiet. Nothing to report."

"Good. Thank you. You're dismissed."

They left to rest before their afternoon shift, and Mal'ik found himself in front of another door he didn't want to enter. He considered standing outside of it until Oliver came out on his own. The man was unerringly punctual. He didn't need Mal'ik prodding him along, and that wasn't Mal'ik's job anyway.

But it *was* Mal'ik's job to provide close protection. And once the day began—which it did at precisely seven o'clock —Mal'ik needed to be closer. So he knocked on the door briskly, opened it too, and stepped into Oliver's rooms.

The scents of the night hit him like a punch to the gut, and he froze on the threshold: the sting of the drink he had brought, the clean linen of Oliver's baseline smell, the wood shaving and musk of the oil Mal'ik had used to open Oliver up. And layering over it all like a quilt, the earthiness of Oliver's desperate arousal mixed with the aggression of Mal'ik's.

Mal'ik swallowed and closed the door behind him but didn't dare go any farther into the room.

"Good morning." Oliver stepped out of the bedroom, dressed immaculately, with not a golden hair out of place, and smelling like absolutely nothing. He didn't wait for Mal'ik to respond, just motioned to the door. "Shall we?"

Mal'ik nodded and led the way out into the hall and to the dining room. Oliver carried on like any other morning, even pointing out the weeds growing in the pot outside the entrance to the dining room that he would have expected to be pulled by then.

Mal'ik wasn't surprised by Oliver's blithe disregard for what they had done last night. He wasn't even disappointed. He had given Oliver something he had needed—and felt lucky for the opportunity to do so—and that was that. And if such a dismissal twisted at his heart, coming from a man who had even asked for his advice and opinions, then that was entirely his own problem.

And so the day went.

Mal'ik escorted Oliver to meetings. Oliver drove hard bargains, and pushed politicians further than they had been prepared to be pushed, even though word of Oliver's ruthlessness had spread among them by that point. And then Mal'ik escorted Oliver out of meetings and tried not to be too amused by Oliver's snide and self-satisfied comments about how the previous meeting had gone.

Oliver was a force of nature, and he knew it. Mal'ik found it hard not to be drawn to that sort of competent self-satisfaction.

Toward the tail end of Oliver's conversation with the transportation minister, the time for the afternoon guards to be exchanged with the evening guards came, and Patrick accompanied them. He stepped beside Mal'ik and tilted his head toward him so they could speak while still keeping an eye on the windows and doorways.

"There's been a change of plans for the meeting after this," Patrick told him. The next meeting was with Governor Tesh of Southern Tava. Mal'ik had been

dreading it all day. "The governor has requested the presence of Emissary Serihk and his consultant Bryant
Harrison."

Mal'ik frowned. He knew Emissary Serihk was here
and that he'd been conducting his own meetings with the
Klah'Eel. He was already due to meet with Oliver on his
own tomorrow, though Mal'ik had found it odd they hadn't
arranged a meeting earlier. Mal'ik wasn't a politician by
any means, but he knew Oliver and Serihk were two of the
most powerful players in this particular game, and from
what he had seen of Oliver and what he knew of Serihk,
there was going to be tension between their two goals. He
didn't think the governor as a third player was a good sign.

"And has requested that they meet on Emissary
Serihk's ship," Patrick continued.

"No." The word was out of Mal'ik's mouth before he'd
fully considered it. His gut was against it. It gave Serihk too
much high ground in any conversation.

Patrick glanced at him, and the corner of his mouth
tugged down in a frown. "I'm not sure that's our call,
Mal'ik."

"It is if I consider it a security risk."

"Do you?"

He didn't. Serihk's security system was legendary
among those in the security industry. A ship had fewer
entrances to worry about and no windows. And Mal'ik
didn't doubt Serihk's integrity. He wasn't worried that this
was a trap or an assassination attempt. He just didn't like
the idea of Oliver sitting in a negotiation under the magni-
fying glass of Serihk's sensors, having his every movement
calculated and analyzed. Oliver was good at this game, but
Serihk had been playing it for a lot longer.

"No," he had to admit. "We'll let Turner decide."

Patrick nodded and stayed silent by his side for a few

minutes longer while the transportation minister attempted to drone on but kept getting interrupted by Oliver's sharp retorts.

Mal'ik knew what was coming when he saw Patrick lick his lips out of the corner of his eye and then open his mouth.

"Word got back to me about something."

"Did it?" Mal'ik kept his face neutral and his voice almost flat. This wasn't a conversation he wanted to have. He wasn't going to make it easy on Patrick no matter how long they had known each other.

Patrick scowled. "Don't be like that, Mal'ik. Is it true?"

"Is what true?"

Patrick's pale skin tinged pink. The man had seen some of the most brutal and bloody fights a man could, but he'd never been good at talking about anything related to sex. Not that it had come up often in their friendship. He pitched his voice low. "Did you sleep with Turner last night?"

For a petty second, Mal'ik wanted to say no. Because he hadn't slept with Oliver. He hadn't even been allowed to hold Oliver once they had finished. Or clean him up. Or kiss him good night. Oliver had run from the bed to the shower, smelling of panic, and hadn't looked back. But that didn't need to be aired.

"Yes."

Patrick inhaled sharply as if Mal'ik's answer surprised him even though he had obviously known what it would be. "Well, I didn't expect that."

"Neither did I." Mal'ik didn't make stupid decisions like entanglements with clients. And a man like Oliver didn't look twice at a man like him unless it was in horror or distaste. He wondered which of those improbable obstacles shocked Patrick more, that Mal'ik wanted Oliver or that Oliver wanted Mal'ik. *Had wanted.* Mal'ik had no idea if Oliver still did.

"Do you need to be taken off the assignment?" To Patrick's credit, his voice didn't waver when he asked the question. He'd never been one to shirk or hide away from his duty, even when another man might have put friendship first.

"That's up to you," Mal'ik replied. Patrick was second-in-command. If Mal'ik was compromised, it was up to him to see him replaced. Mal'ik didn't want to be taken off the assignment. He didn't want to leave Oliver's protection to anyone else. But that was exactly the sort of thinking that clouded his judgment on the matter.

Patrick didn't answer right away. He turned to Mal'ik and gave him a hard look, then swept his eyes to Oliver, then around the room.

"No, I don't think you do," he finally said. "Not yet, at least."

Mal'ik nodded and something uncoiled in his chest that he hadn't realized had been tightening up. "Alright."

"Take care of yourself, Mal'ik."

Mal'ik frowned. "What's that supposed to mean?"

"I don't know. Just that, I guess." Patrick shrugged. He nodded toward Oliver. "I don't think anything good can come out of a man like that."

A fierce indignation flared to life in Mal'ik's chest, so strong he instinctively clamped down on it.

Before he could think of a more reasonable reply, Patrick was already continuing. "I'm going to go check the path to the Emissary's ship. Let me know what Turner decides." Patrick left Mal'ik to wrestle with more feelings than he had any right or reason to have.

After several more minutes, Oliver and the transportation minister stood and shook hands. Oliver scrubbed his eyes once the door closed behind the minister, leaving them alone in the room.

"That man is exhausting," he groused, stretching his hands into the air as he walked back to Mal'ik. He dropped into a chair in front of him, lounging on it halfway slid out in a way he never did when there were politicians around.

"I'm told that's the general consensus."

"Maybe I should give him a call when my insomnia flares up." Oliver dropped his head back against the chair. "I'm sure hearing him spout meaningless words at a snail's pace would have me snoring in under an hour."

"You snore?" Mal'ik raised his eyebrows, having a hard time picturing anything as undignified as a snore emitting from Oliver's refined nose and mouth.

Oliver sat up at that, and that refined mouth pinched. "I wouldn't know. I'm asleep, and there's never been anyone around to tell me."

Perhaps because he kicked people out of his bed before they even had a chance to try to stay. Though judging by Oliver's tightness last night and lack of lube, not many people ever made it into Oliver's bed in the first place. Mal'ik almost grimaced. He shouldn't have taken the conversation here. Before he could think of how to salvage it, though, Oliver stood.

"Well, one more meeting, so let's get this over with." He started walking toward the exit, the lines of his body sharp and straight again. "I'll give Governor Tesh one thing—he won't be boring."

"There's been a change of plans," Mal'ik said before Oliver reached the door. "The governor has requested the meeting take place on Emissary Serihk's ship, with the Emissary and his human consultant present."

Oliver stopped, then turned to him slowly, lips pressed

together and brow furrowed. He crossed his arms. "Well, I don't like that."

Mal'ik hadn't thought he would and stayed silent as Oliver mulled over his next move.

"Tesh must think the Emissary will be an ally to him." Oliver didn't look at Mal'ik as he spoke. Instead, his eyes bored into the carpet beside Mal'ik's feet. "And he's gotten to him before I could. And if the Emissary's allowed him to do that, it's because he's already decided I'm the enemy." His face briefly twisted into a furious expression. "I never wanted that damn qesh here."

"The request was last minute," Mal'ik said. "I can refuse it on security grounds."

Oliver's eyes flickered up to meet his, and he gave a half smile. "And help me save face?"

"Yes."

For a moment, Oliver's expression looked the way it had when they'd sat on the couch last night. Soft and open, with a sweet, genuine smile. Then he shook his head.

"No. Unfortunately, that would be transparent. We'll go there now and do this meeting or I'll be admitting they got me on the back foot. And I think you know me well enough by now to know that's not acceptable."

Mal'ik felt a little pulse of satisfaction to realize that he did know Oliver well enough to know that. "I understand."

Mal'ik led Oliver through the door—Oliver usually let Mal'ik enter and leave rooms first, though he insisted on being first into a meeting—and through the arcades to the hangar.

Concern niggled at Mal'ik's mind, though, and he couldn't help clarifying as they walked, "You're familiar with the Emissary's security system?"

"You mean his eavesdropping and spying system?"

Mal'ik chuckled. "Yes."

"I'm familiar." Oliver sighed. "I looked into getting one myself, but the neural links haven't yet been developed for human brains."

Mal'ik smiled at the disappointment in Oliver's voice. He wasn't surprised the man was interested in a system that gave him omnipotence, even if it was just over a small space. Then he continued, "He'll be recording you. And he'll rewatch the meeting afterward to spot any tells he might have missed."

"I know, Mal'ik." Oliver looked up at him with an amused smile playing over his lips. "It's exactly what I'd do. I'll be fine."

Mal'ik nodded and looked forward again, feeling the faint heat of an embarrassed blush on the back of his neck. Oliver did not need Mal'ik fussing over him.

"You seem to know quite a bit about Emissary Serihk," Oliver said after a moment. "Are you acquainted with him personally?"

Mal'ik hesitated. Something in Oliver's tone put him on edge. "A little. I am close with his bodyguard."

"I see. And do you like Emissary Serihk?"

"I only know him in certain contexts."

"That's not what I asked."

Mal'ik glanced down at Oliver to see him staring straight ahead, face placid and shoulders stiff. He cursed the scent-neutralizing cream that kept him from sniffing out whatever was going on in Oliver's clearly complicated mind. "Yes, I do."

Oliver nodded, and they didn't say anything more until they got to the hangar and stood in front of Serihk's understated ship. Mal'ik had no idea what he had said wrong or what conclusion Oliver had come to. But the silence was so heavy, Mal'ik had to swallow before he could move his tongue enough to break it.

"Because of the security system, I don't need to be in the same room during your meeting," he said. "I can give you some privacy, or I can attend. It's your decision."

"I'd prefer the privacy."

The immediacy of Oliver's reply hit something tender in Mal'ik's chest that it shouldn't have. Maybe he should give serious consideration to Patrick's question of whether he should be taken off this assignment.

As they walked up the gangway, the front door slid open to reveal an opulently decorated welcoming hall with dark paneled walls and a plush carpet. Standing in the room, ready to greet them as they entered, was Emissary Serihk—skin pale, hands behind his back, a polite smile on his face—and a human man Mal'ik didn't recognize—bearded, shorter and younger than Serihk, but more muscular than any politician Mal'ik had ever met. Behind them both stood the governor of Southern Tava, practically skulking in the shadows.

"Mr. Turner, it's a pleasure to finally meet you." Serihk stepped forward and reached out with one of his elegant hands in a human greeting.

Oliver smiled and shook his hand. "And you as well, Emissary Serihk. Your reputation precedes you."

"As does yours and your family's." Serihk smiled back and then turned to Mal'ik. "And Captain Mal'ik, it's a pleasure to see you again."

Mal'ik dipped his head. "And you, sir."

Serihk waved the human man forward. "Thank you for sending over those bodyguard recommendations for Mr. Harrison here. It's much appreciated." Mal'ik felt more than saw Oliver's eyes flick over to him.

"Mr. Harrison." Mal'ik nodded to the human in front of him and tried not to look at the human beside him. "I can personally vouch for every one of them. I hope you find someone that suits you."

Harrison guffawed. "If any of them are half as good as Lar'a, I'm sure I'll be fine."

"That's a high standard, but they'll meet it." Mal'ik smiled genuinely, surprised by the casual gruffness of the man's voice. It gave Mal'ik the impression that he spoke with an equal, rather than the elites he spent so much time surrounded by. Harrison had a different accent than Oliver, more rounded, and he didn't hit his consonants quite as crisply.

Serihk turned back to Oliver. "Mr. Turner, please meet my consultant, Bryant Harrison. He'll be joining us for any meetings."

"A pleasure to meet you, Mr. Harrison." Oliver's tone sounded impressively genuine, even though Mal'ik didn't doubt that Oliver wasn't getting any pleasure from any of this. Oliver also didn't extend his hand to Harrison like Serihk had to him, but Mal'ik didn't know enough about Human culture to know if that was a snub.

"Good to meet you too, Mr. Turner." Harrison definitely wasn't from a political background. He didn't have the knack of pretending to be impressed by someone that he wasn't. Mal'ik glanced down at Oliver and wasn't surprised to see a perfectly polite and uncracked mask.

Serihk stepped back and swept his arm out to the governor behind them. "And, of course, you know Governor Tesh." Oliver and the governor nodded to each other. "And with that, I believe introductions are done. I've had the study arranged for our meeting. Will you be joining us, Captain Mal'ik?"

"No, sir."

"In that case, Lar'a is in the gym if you'd like to join her. I'm sure you remember the way?"

"Yes, sir."

Mal'ik looked at Oliver one last time before they parted, but Oliver was already walking away, following Harrison down the hallway across from them. Mal'ik watched him go, feeling the urge to follow. Oliver wasn't in any danger, but he wasn't in friendly territory, and Mal'ik should be at his back.

But Oliver didn't want him there, so Mal'ik left to find Lar'a.

But as he turned down a hallway, he was surprised to come face-to-face with a very different klah'eel woman. "Teav?"

Teav's eyes widened for just a moment before she marshaled herself. "Captain Mal'ik."

"What are you doing here?"

Teav's expression didn't change but a curl of embarrassment twisted over the air to him. "Nothing." Mal'ik raised an eyebrow, and Teav gave a little huff. "I just wanted to talk to Lar'a about some data she sent over. I wanted to clarify a few points."

Mal'ik raised the second eyebrow as the corner of his lips twitched. "Mm-hmm."

The smell of embarrassment intensified, and Teav scowled and moved to walk past him. "Excuse me. I need to get going."

Mal'ik let her go and managed to keep from chuckling until she was out of earshot.

He found Lar'a with a heavy-laden barbell over her shoulders and a young human girl counting out her squat reps. When Lar'a caught sight of Mal'ik in the doorway, she grinned and heaved the barbell back onto the rack.

"Mal'ik! I was wondering if you'd get away to join us."

As Lar'a strode over, the coil of unhappiness that had still been gathering in Mal'ik's chest at being sent away loosened. An hour surrounded by weights with an old friend was better than watching diplomats snipe at each other, no matter who they were.

"Here I am. I also just saw Teav?" Mal'ik let the insinuation trail off and was not surprised when Lar'a's grin turned roguish.

"She just stopped by to talk about some data. It probably could have been a data tablet message, but…" Lar'a shrugged in a faux casual way. Mal'ik had known Lar'a long enough to know that the but was "but if she just happened to stop by while I was showing off with a barbell, then that's even better."

"Right. Well, you'll have to make do with me now. I can't lift with you, though. I'm still on duty."

"That's fine. You can spot for us." Lar'a waved over the young girl, who had been perched on a bench. "Astrid, this is Captain Mal'ik. He taught *me* to use a gatlung."

"That's not true." Mal'ik snorted. He looked down at the girl. "She was already very good when I met her."

"You made me better." Lar'a pointed at him. "Mal'ik, this is Astrid Harrison. She'll be one of the first humans to be trained by the Gat'Raph."

"Harrison?"

Astrid grinned. "You probably met my dad."

"Bryant," Lar'a supplied.

Mal'ik took a moment to rearrange his conception of the rough-looking man by Serihk's side so that it could include him being the father of a young daughter. Then the second half of Lar'a's introduction caught up with him.

"The Gat'Raph?"

"They're starting an experimental mixed regiment of humans and klah'eel," Astrid said with the air of someone reciting something they were very proud of. "I'll be one of the first human recruits."

"That's good." Mal'ik nodded and thought of the years he'd fought beside Patrick. "Some of my greatest comrades were humans. And our empire needs more integration between the species."

"That's what Lar'a and Serihk always say."

"And that's why we're friends." Lar'a clapped her hands. "Come on, rest time's over. We've got a lot more sets to get through."

They fell into the easy rhythms of a workout, with Mal'ik as a full-time spotter. Lar'a had written an aggressive workout on the large screen on the wall, and Mal'ik was privately glad he had a solid excuse for not participating. Though, if he was starting to shy away from workouts, it meant he needed to do them more. He'd make Patrick step up their training regimens once these talks were over and the job was done.

And Oliver left.

Mal'ik pushed the thought away. Yes, Oliver would leave in a week or so when this was all done. And everything would go back to the way it was before. Mal'ik had never had a problem with the way things had been before. Things were barely any different right now.

He'd only met Oliver a few days ago. And yes, Oliver made his heart race and chest warm. And yes, he made Mal'ik feel…worthwhile. Like he was more than just the soldier he'd always been. And yes, Mal'ik had fucked him, and it had been amazing. But none of it changed anything. It certainly hadn't changed anything for Oliver.

"What's eating you?" Lar'a looked up at him, sniffing with a scrunched nose. She was lying on her back on a bench, hands on the barbell that Mal'ik was about to help her lift off the rack.

"Nothing." Mal'ik shook his head and braced to lift the weight before Lar'a could press for a better answer. "Ready?"

The workout slowed after the better part of an hour, moving into a cooldown and stretching phase that didn't need Mal'ik's help. So he sat on one of the benches and twirled a little two-pound weight in his hand.

Lar'a brought her arm across her chest to stretch her shoulders. "Job's been quiet so far."

Mal'ik nodded. "Yeah."

Astrid glanced between them. "You guys don't like it, do you?"

"Nope." Lar'a shook her head. "I've been hearing things about that new Resistance leader."

"So have I." Mal'ik sighed and set the weight down. "Ethan mentioned him in one of his letters recently. Said he's even more idealistic than most, and not in a good way."

"Ethan?" Lar'a repeated. "You still hear from him?"

"He sends me letters every few months. Lets me know how he's doing."

Lar'a snorted. "And people think you're scary." She looked at Astrid. "Mal'ik pulled Ethan and his dad out of a burning building back during the occupation. I guess little Ethan developed some hero worship."

"He's not little anymore," Mal'ik pointed out. Ethan was well and truly an adult now, and Mal'ik had a feeling he wasn't staying as far from trouble as he should. Then again, Mal'ik hadn't been to Southern Tava in years, but when he was there, it was impossible to get too far from trouble.

"Are they human?" Astrid asked, frowning up at him.

Mal'ik frowned back. "Yes. You sound surprised."

Astrid blushed a little but pushed on. "I didn't know any klah'eel helped any humans back then."

Lar'a scoffed. "Our job was to protect the people. Most of those people were humans. But so were the attackers."

"After the invasion was over, the violence came from the Resistance," Mal'ik explained. He didn't go into details about how much violence or of what sort. The girl may be going to join the Gat'Raph, but she didn't need those images yet.

Astrid didn't look entirely convinced, but she shrugged and went back to her stretching. Before Mal'ik and Lar'a could continue their discussion, the screen on the wall beeped.

Mal'ik hadn't realized how much strain had dropped off his shoulders from the pleasant company and soothing workout routine until he read the message that the meeting was over and Mal'ik was needed back in the entrance hall to escort Oliver out.

"Come for drinks tonight?" Lar'a asked as he stood.

"I'm on close protection duty."

"Yes, but you're off in the evening, aren't you?" Lar'a asked. "We'll be leaving as soon as this is resolved, and I don't know when we'll be coming back to Tava. Serihk will want to see you."

"And you should meet my dad. I think you'll like him," Astrid piped up.

Mal'ik had a feeling he would like her dad. He was already warming up to her.

"They don't have to be alcoholic drinks," Lar'a added.

Mal'ik sighed and shook his head. "Maybe. It was good to see you, Lar'a. And to meet you, Astrid."

"Bye!" Astrid called as he left, and he smiled to himself as he walked down the hall. It had been a long time since he'd interacted with anyone not yet into adulthood. He'd forgotten how much hope and optimism they carried around without realizing it. He hadn't interacted with anyone of the optimistic sort in years either.

Until Oliver.

Prissy and astringent as he was, Oliver was the most aggressively optimistic person Mal'ik had ever met. He insisted on better, thoroughly believed better was possible, and implicitly believed in his own ability to attain it. It was oddly inspiring.

But Oliver didn't look optimistic when Mal'ik found him in the entry hall. He was frowning hard and standing ramrod straight. When he caught sight of Mal'ik, he turned on his heel.

"Finally. Let's go."

Mal'ik caught up to him before he could storm down the gangway without protection, and they hurried through the hangar and back into the hallways of the estate. Mal'ik glanced down at Oliver as they walked. The human hadn't been in a good mood before the meeting, and Mal'ik didn't need to smell him to know the mood was worse now.

About halfway back to their rooms, Oliver opened his mouth and turned to Mal'ik. But then he closed it and looked away.

After a few more moments, Mal'ik found himself opening his own mouth. "What happened in the meeting?"

He didn't have the right to ask the question. It wasn't his business. But he did anyway.

Oliver's lips twisted as he shook his head. "Nothing."

Mal'ik took the lie in silence even though it stung like his prosthetic interfacing with his nerves every morning. Painful, but necessary. It was good that Oliver would put distance between them, seeing as Mal'ik seemed incapable of it.

But then Oliver sighed, and his shoulders slumped. "Nothing important," he amended.

They arrived at Oliver's rooms, and Oliver turned to face him. But he kept his hazel eyes on some point over Mal'ik's shoulder instead of meeting his gaze. Again he opened his mouth only to close it, and Mal'ik was left to break the silence.

"Can I do anything…" Mal'ik hesitated, unsure whether to use Oliver's given name or his family name.

But Oliver was already shaking his head before he could decide. "No. Nothing." He spun back to his door and input the keycode with brisk taps. "Have a good night, Captain Mal'ik."

Mal'ik's title hit him like a blow, but he took that in silence too. He swallowed around the hurt to get the reply out. "Good night, Turner."

He saw Oliver's shoulders hunch up for just a moment, and then the door swung shut.

Mal'ik stifled a groan, rolled his neck, and turned to face the hallway. Once the night guards came to relieve him, he would take Lar'a up on her drinks offer.

WHEN MAL'IK ARRIVED at Serihk's infamous ship, Bryant Harrison was standing in the entryway to greet him. The human put his hands on his hips and gave him a grin, surprisingly warm for how little they'd interacted so far.

"So you did manage to escape." He stepped aside to welcome Mal'ik in and chuckled. "I hear it was Turner who made a break for it earlier, though. Sounds like he practically ran down the gangway."

"He was eager to leave." Mal'ik tamped down a swell of the same indignation that had arisen when Patrick had said something cruel about Oliver. Neither Bryant nor Patrick had meant any offense. Not to Mal'ik, at least.

"You don't say. I think he was eager to leave as soon as he got here." Bryant waved for Mal'ik to follow him down a hall. "Lar'a decided last minute she had to introduce Astrid to someone. I hope you don't mind hanging out with just Serihk and me."

"Not at all." Mal'ik was a little disappointed to have missed Lar'a but was curious how this human consultant fitted into things. And it was always interesting to see Serihk without his diplomat mask.

Mal'ik followed Bryant into the elegant dining room. A few bottles and an abandoned glass that must have been Lar'a's sat on the table, and Serihk sat across from the doorway.

"Glad you could make it, Captain Mal'ik." Emissary Serihk raised his glass to him. "How is your arm?"

Serihk had been involved in the incident that had taken Mal'ik's arm. He'd also been the one to commission his prosthetic for him. He always asked about it, and for a while, Mal'ik hadn't known whether the question was prompted by guilt or by wanting to make Mal'ik feel he owed him. As the years had passed, Mal'ik had become more certain it was the guilt.

"Better than ever," Mal'ik replied, to assuage it as much as he could. It hadn't been Serihk's fault.

"Good." Serihk leaned back in his chair and raised an eyebrow. "And how's the assignment? He was out of here rather quickly today."

Oliver's hasty retreat seemed a popular topic of conversation tonight. Mal'ik poured himself some of the purple liquid from the bottle in the center of the table. It was a Qeshian brew he didn't often have, but he liked the floral notes. Sipping it now, it reminded him of the way Oliver smelled.

"I noticed." Mal'ik settled into a chair once he had his drink. "Did something happen?"

"Nothing at all." Serihk shook his head, and Bryant laughed loudly. The human reached over and shoved Serihk's shoulder in a familiar way that made Mal'ik's eyes widen. He didn't think he'd ever seen someone *shove* Emissary Serihk. The most he'd seen was Lar'a giving him an eye roll. But Serihk looked strangely pleased, a slight smile curling his lips and some pink and purple swirling just above his collar.

"Serihk's full of shit." Bryant shook his head and looked at Mal'ik. "He was goading Turner the whole meeting."

"I was not."

"You were."

"I was a little."

Bryant leaned over the table to Mal'ik. "He was a lot."

"Well, someone had to put him back in his place." Serihk set his glass down hard, though he looked exasperated more than angry. "The Klah'Eel are excellent warriors, I'll give them that, but they're *terrible* negotiators. They were letting Turner have the run of the place."

Bryant scowled. "And you think they're any better at government? You think that that Governor Tesh should be in charge instead?"

"He's at least an elected official." Serihk pointed at Bryant with one of the fingers from the hand on his glass before taking a small sip. "He lives in the area and he knows its needs."

"He knows his own needs, at least," Mal'ik cut in in a low voice.

"Exactly." Bryant nodded. "There's something about him I don't like."

Mal'ik felt another burst of affinity for this human. There was something he didn't like about that governor either, but he hadn't known if it was the way his nostrils had flared eagerly as he'd leaned toward Oliver that first meeting in the courtyard.

"What, and you like Turner?" Serihk scoffed as though the idea was absurd. "You would hand the planet over to a Human oligarch to get out of dealing with a little social unrest?"

"I wouldn't call the Resistance 'a little social unrest.'" Mal'ik frowned.

Serihk grimaced. "Granted."

"And also, I don't think Turner's proposals are half bad." Bryant jutted his chin out at Serihk. "I'm going to take another look at them now that I've met him."

"Well, we've already talked about what happened the last time a planet thought Oliver Turner's proposals weren't half bad." Serihk cocked his own chin and drummed his fingers along the sides of his glass. But his skin tinged orange when Bryant's face darkened.

"Yes, *you* did, didn't you?" Bryant scowled at him, and Mal'ik was surprised to see Serihk drop his eyes with something like shame. "That was cruel."

"It was effective," Serihk replied crisply. "He'll be off-balance tomorrow. We'll need that opening to remind the Klah'Eel delegation that they don't need the Turner family."

"What was cruel?" Mal'ik demanded. His gut clenched with unease. He should have pushed harder to stay with Oliver in the meeting. He'd known Oliver hadn't been among friends. If Mal'ik had been there, perhaps Oliver would have talked to him about it afterward. Instead of sending him away with "*Have a good night, Captain Mal'ik.*"

Bryant looked pointedly at Serihk, and Serihk sighed. "I reminded him of a particularly cataclysmic failure of his. One that I'm sure involved a great deal of personal discomfort for him. And familial strain."

"Personal discomfort," Bryant muttered. He shook his head and turned to Mal'ik. "He was blown up. Well, the building he was in was. He was probably the target. He was buried in the rubble for days."

"A day and a half," Serihk murmured, as though he just couldn't help making the correction.

"I'm sure it felt like days to him," Bryant snapped.

Mal'ik barely heard them.

He couldn't stop seeing Oliver in his mind's eye, bloody and dirty, trapped in some small, tight, dark space between rough stone and metal. He'd have screamed until his throat was hoarse, and then what? Cried, sobbed, stared despondently into the darkness?

No, he'd have fought and struggled. He'd have scraped at the rocks until he tore off every fingernail. Mal'ik was sure of it.

"He almost died of the infection—"

"Infection?" Mal'ik interrupted Bryant as he came back to the expensive dining room of Serihk's ship.

"He had some open wounds." Bryant nodded. "And most of the people around him had been crushed. He was covered in blood, mud, and shit when they found him."

He said it in such a matter-of-fact tone, Mal'ik was certain he'd seen some things himself. Mal'ik had too. He'd seen his own bloody stump where his right arm had once been. But he was a soldier. He was *supposed* to see those sorts of things. A man like Oliver wasn't.

"What prompted the attack?" Mal'ik asked.

"It was a similar situation to this one," Serihk replied. His tone had sobered, and Mal'ik appreciated that at least. "Turner family trying to exploit a resource-rich but socially broken planet. Weak local government. Violent resistance organization. Most of the leaders at the summit were killed and the plan was scuppered. I believe the mercenary corporation owned by Turner's stepfather swooped in. He made trillions, and the Turner family made nothing."

Mal'ik stood. "I have to go."

Serihk winced. "I admit, it wasn't the kindest thing to bring up."

Bryant shook his head, but his mouth twisted into a fond smile, and the smell that wafted off him was almost saccharine. He placed a hand on the nape of Serihk's neck and rubbed his thumb over the skin once before pulling his hand back. "You were trying to win."

Purple and pink crawled up Serihk's neck, and the smell of affection swirled through the air. Whatever it was between them was nothing Mal'ik had been expecting. He felt a stab of jealousy. He had someone that he needed to be comforting, even if that someone didn't want it.

Bryant sighed and stood. "I'll walk you out, Mal'ik."

"Thank you for the drink." Mal'ik nodded to Serihk before he left. "It was good to see you again."

"And you, Captain Mal'ik."

He followed Bryant back out into the hall and toward the ship's exit. Mal'ik turned to say his goodbyes when the door opened, but Bryant gestured for him to continue. Bryant followed him out of the ship and down the gangway until they'd reached the ground outside. Finally, Mal'ik turned around with a frown.

Bryant gave him a crooked smile and waved back toward the ship. "Serihk is definitely listening. But he can't hear us out here."

"I see." Mal'ik raised his eyebrows. "Can't hear us talk about what?"

"You seemed pretty upset back there."

"Did I?"

Bryant snorted. "No. Not obviously, I guess. Still. I think you were upset about what Serihk did to Turner. Or you were upset about what happened to him?"

"What happened to him was a terrible thing." Mal'ik kept his voice calm even while his heart thudded. It *was* a terrible thing. And it happened to *Oliver*. And he hadn't known about it. "I do have to go now. It was nice to meet you."

Bryant stared at him with shrewd eyes for a moment longer and then nodded. "Yeah, you too. I'll see you around."

Mal'ik watched him turn back around to head to the gangway and then spun on his heel and strode back toward his rooms. As soon as he left the hanger, he called Patrick on his earpiece.

"What's up?" Patrick asked, and his voice sounded sleepy. He'd always been early to bed.

"Why didn't I know Oliver Turner had been targeted before?"

"What are you talking about? You did know." There was a grunt on the other end, some rustling, and then Patrick's voice came in clearer. "It was all in the briefing."

Mal'ik stopped as he thought back. It *had* been in the briefing. Turner had had a few attempts on his life and a few attempted kidnappings, which was standard for someone with the kind of money he came from. The most serious attempt had been a bombing. Mal'ik remembered reading that. And he remembered handpicking bomb experts for his team, setting up protocols for all packages, and personnel specifically to sweep for explosives.

Mal'ik had known about the explosion, and he had prepared appropriately for it. The information just hadn't been mentally filed into anywhere that meant it *mattered* to him.

"Mal'ik, what's wrong?" Patrick interrupted his thinking, and Mal'ik resumed his walking.

"Nothing. You're right. It slipped my mind. Have a good night."

"Mal'ik—"

But Mal'ik ended the call.

Chapter Five

"GOOD NIGHT, TURNER."

Oliver lay in bed with the lights off and his eyes wide open, replaying every place where the evening had gone more and more wrong, all culminating with that formal, *"Good night, Turner."*

No, actually, it had culminated with him walking across the hallway to knock on Mal'ik's door under the inquisitive eyes of the night guards, only to have one of them tell him that Mal'ik had gone out. It wasn't until he'd felt the bloom of embarrassment and pathetic jealousy that he'd remembered he wasn't wearing his scent cream and that the guards could smell all the feelings on him.

He'd been too mortified to manage anything but a terse shake of the head and a quick "no" when they'd asked if they should call Mal'ik before slamming the door shut again.

Oliver rolled over and pulled the covers up to his ears.

His foolishness had started with that petty bout of insecurity when he'd learned Mal'ik knew Emissary Serihk. As though Mal'ik had abandoned him or tricked him. As though Mal'ik was anything more than his temporary bodyguard. And as though his relationship with Oliver had anything to do with his relationship with Serihk or vice versa.

He didn't know if Serihk had sensed the distance between them or if he'd already been planning to drive a wedge between Oliver and his bodyguard, but his work had been transparent. And effective. Treat the only person on the ship in Oliver's corner as though he were actually in Serihk's. Emphasize and accentuate Oliver's isolation. Oliver had to hand it to the qesh, it's what he would have done.

And yes, Oliver would have even thrown Serihk's worst day back in his face, too, if that had been an option for him. But if Serihk had had a day like the one Oliver had had spent trapped and suffocating—Oliver rolled onto his back and flung his covers back down to his waist—if Serihk had had a day like that, Oliver didn't know of it.

And so Serihk had wiped the floor with him. It hadn't even been a negotiation. It had barely been a meeting. It had just been Serihk telling him—with a lot of political words and barely veiled barbs—that he was here to stop Oliver and there was nothing Oliver could do about it.

Oliver swung his legs out of bed and scrubbed his hands over his face.

His only comfort was that his father hadn't been there to see it.

He could still *feel* the disdainful fury in the look his father had given him as he lay in the hospital, every inch of him stinging with antiseptic. He could hear the blame in his father's voice as he told him that the deal had fallen through. That the Wate Group had struck a deal of their own.

His father hadn't been there to tell him that he was

going to live or that he would get to keep his leg. He hadn't been there to tell him he was glad he was alive or that he hoped he got better soon.

He had come to the hospital to tell him that the deal had fallen through.

But *this* deal hadn't fallen through yet. Emissary Serihk may have declared himself an adversary, but he certainly hadn't won anything yet.

Oliver shook himself and then stood and headed back to the shower. He was Oliver Turner. He was the youngest —and soon to be once again favorite—son of the magnificently powerful Turner family dynasty. A trumped-up bureaucratic diplomat wasn't going to get in his way.

Just before he'd stepped into the bathroom, hands already on his shirt to pull it off, he heard a knock on the door. He paused. It was the middle of the night. Anything urgent and that knock would have been more like a bang. Another soft knock sounded.

"Turner, are you awake?"

Oliver's heart jumped into his throat at the deep rumble of Mal'ik's voice through the door. He quickly stuffed it back down into his chest cavity. Captain Mal'ik was not here for a late-night tryst. For one, he didn't seem like to type to make booty calls, and for two, no one was going to want to jump back into bed with Oliver after his abysmal behavior last night, flying out of bed like a bat out of hell.

"Yes," Oliver called back. He padded to the door and pulled it open. Mal'ik stood there looking grim-faced, his heavy brows pinched, the unblemished side of his lips downturned, and the other pulling on his scars. "What's wrong?"

"You were looking for me?" Mal'ik stepped onto the threshold, filling up the doorway with his bulk.

"It wasn't important." Oliver shook his head. It hadn't been. Oliver hadn't even been sure what he was going to ask of Mal'ik if he had been there. *Please sit with me quietly so I don't feel so alone?*

"I want to come in and sweep the room." Mal'ik moved forward so that Oliver had to step back and let him in. "I should have done it earlier."

Bewildered, Oliver shut the door and turned to put his back against it as he watched Mal'ik go through the same ritual he had when Oliver had first arrived. Pulling open cabinets and drawers and peering under furniture. Looking into the vents.

Oliver didn't have a klah'eel's smell, and he couldn't claim to know Mal'ik well enough to know his mannerisms, but something about the tense set of his shoulders and jaw —and the fact that he'd barged into Oliver's room in the middle of the night—itched at him.

"Is something wrong?" Oliver asked again.

"No."

"I don't believe you."

Mal'ik closed the closet in the study and walked back across the foyer to stand in front of Oliver. He looked down at him seriously, and Oliver shifted under his gaze.

"Nothing is wrong, Oliver," he said, and Oliver felt a flicker of relief to hear him say his name again. "I'm just here to keep it that way."

He walked into the bedroom, and Oliver followed him. Oliver leaned against the doorjamb and watched Mal'ik sweep the room thoroughly and steadily.

Oliver bit his lip. "Where were you this evening?" he asked. He knew he didn't have a right to, but Mal'ik being in here made him feel like he did. "When I was looking for you."

Mal'ik paused with Oliver's wardrobe open. That

pause made Oliver's stomach drop out, and he crossed his arms over his chest. He was just opening his mouth to ask again in a different tone when Mal'ik replied.

"Serihk's ship."

Oliver winced and pulled his crossed arms tighter into his chest. Why was that so upsetting to him? What did it matter that Mal'ik had friends or that those friends might be the same people that had just gutted him a few hours ago, opposed him, and wanted to stomp all over everything he was so desperately working for? Mal'ik wasn't his teammate, and this wasn't a betrayal.

Mal'ik closed the wardrobe doors and turned back around to face him. But Oliver couldn't see his expression; he was too busy staring at one of the walls. The same wall Mal'ik had pressed him up against last night, actually. He flushed and diverted his attention to a different wall.

"It was cruel of him to bring up what he did." Mal'ik walked across the room and stood in front of Oliver, close enough to touch but not reaching out.

Oliver bristled. So that's what this was about. "It was strategy."

He narrowed his eyes at Mal'ik. So he knew then, about those hours, that day Oliver spent nearly drowning in mud and offal. Panic rose in his chest as he thought about it, and he shoved it back down.

"Are you alright?" Mal'ik tilted his head but didn't reach for him, and it was a good thing, or Oliver might have lashed out.

Instead, he just stepped back. "I'm fine," he snapped. "I don't need you here checking to see if I've devolved into a gibbering mess because someone said something mean to me."

"That's not what I'm doing."

"Well, whatever you're doing, are you done yet?"

Oliver jerked his head toward the door to his quarters. "I'd like to get back to bed."

Mal'ik nodded slowly. "I'm done. Good night, Oliver."

Oliver's breath caught in his throat at Mal'ik's tone and the sound of his name. Steady, unbothered, unfooled maybe by Oliver's prickliness. He wanted to take back his words and ask Mal'ik to stay instead. He bit his tongue.

When Mal'ik was halfway across the foyer, Oliver released it to choke out, "He never forgave me."

Mal'ik footsteps stopped. The silence stretched. "Who never forgave you for what?"

"My father." Oliver hung his head. He'd never said the words. Not to anyone. Everyone in the Turners' orbit had known, but no one had ever said it. "My father never forgave me for losing that opportunity to Andrew Wate."

Oliver still had his back to Mal'ik, but he heard the big man's heavy footsteps advance on him. "Who is Andrew Wate and why the fuck does he matter?"

"He's the man my mother left us for." Oliver wanted to sink to the ground as all his childhood and present hurts rose to the surface. A mother who had abandoned him, a father who was disappointed in him, no one had ever—

Oliver sucked in a shaky breath and halted his thoughts before they could spiral to somewhere he'd gone enough times.

"Oh, Oliver." Mal'ik wrapped his arms around him from behind and pulled him back against his chest. Oliver let his legs give out, knowing Mal'ik could hold his weight. Mal'ik's tusks scraped against his scalp as Mal'ik nuzzled into his hair. "You didn't deserve that. You didn't deserve any of that. You still don't."

Oliver swallowed the lump in his throat and wiped away the few tears that had gathered in the corners of his eyes. "My father's finally given me this second chance. I've worked my fucking ass off for this chance. I'm not going to ruin it, and I'm not going to let Emissary fucking Serihk ruin it for me either."

Mal'ik tightened his arms around Oliver and pressed a kiss to his temple. "You don't need to prove anything to anyone, Oliver, but..." He sighed and kissed his other temple. "But I understand needing approval from the people that matter."

Oliver closed his eyes and let out a sigh that came out more like a sob. "Thank you." For not making him justify or explain himself. For not telling him that he was a pathetic idiot. For holding him. When was the last time anyone had held him?

He turned his head to bury his nose in Mal'ik's shoulder, where it caved around him, and inhaled deeply. The smell of musk and masculinity filled his nose, along with some other smell that was just Mal'ik that tugged his mind back to last night.

Warmth stirred in his belly.

He licked his lips and then drew the lower one between his teeth. He didn't say anything, knowing his smell was communication enough. He felt rather than heard the growl in Mal'ik's chest.

"Oliver." Mal'ik's warm hand crawled up Oliver's chest to grasp his chin and lift it up. He nudged Oliver's jaw until Oliver was craning his neck around to meet Mal'ik's fiery eyes. He stared up at him, letting Mal'ik's eyes search around his face and his eyes.

Oliver knew exactly what he was going to find there. Desire. Desperate, unabashed desire. "Please."

Mal'ik descended on him before he even finished the word, and Oliver moaned as Mal'ik's mouth met his, fierce and insistent. The big man crushed Oliver against his chest, practically lifting him off the floor and forcing his head around until his neck ached with the position.

The manhandling made Oliver moan, and he let his body go limp and pliant as his cock hardened. "Mal'ik."

"Shh, I've got you." Mal'ik lifted off his lips and turned Oliver's head to the side to kiss down his throat. "I'll take care of you."

Oliver bit off a whimper at the words. He bit his lip and dropped his head back against Mal'ik's shoulder. He flushed, so embarrassed to ask but wanting it desperately. "Say it again."

Mal'ik's hands spasmed where they were grasping his ribs and his hips. "I'll take care of you, Oliver." Mal'ik started undoing the buttons of Oliver's shirt—quick and deft—parting the fabric to expose his chest to the warm Tava air. When Mal'ik's flesh hand reached the bottom of Oliver's torso, he dropped it down to palm Oliver through his pants. "I'm gonna take care of you."

Oliver bucked into Mal'ik's hand and gasped at the pleasure that shot up his spine.

"That's right." Mal'ik undid Oliver's pants and then shoved them down his hips. Mal'ik stepped away from Oliver's back just long enough to pull his shirt off and then crowded up against him again. Mal'ik buried his nose behind Oliver's ear, his tusks scraping sensitive skin and making Oliver shiver, and inhaled deeply. "Fuck, you're intoxicating. You're fucking perfect, Oliver."

Oliver could have cried with the praise. He wanted to be perfect for Mal'ik. He turned toward him, seeking out his lips, and Mal'ik met him with a low moan. He turned Oliver in his arms so that they were face-to-face and swept his tongue into his mouth. Oliver let his mouth drop open, loving the feeling of being invaded as Mal'ik pressed into him. Flashes of memories of other ways Mal'ik had entered him made his cock twitch and rub against the fabric of Mal'ik's clothes.

Mal'ik's clothes.

Oliver flushed as he realized that Mal'ik was still fully clothed, holding Oliver's naked body tight against him. The dirtiness and vulnerability of it made his balls tighten, and he pulled away to look down and see a string of precum hanging between his own cockhead and the front of Mal'ik's pants.

He was too turned on to register disgust. Instead, that smear of his own desire across Mal'ik made him bold. He grabbed the front of Mal'ik's shirt and looked up at him. Mal'ik's orange eyes were focused, his scarred face intense, and Oliver's heart soared to be the focal point of that earnestness.

Oliver yanked him close to slot their mouths together again and pressed their hips together. He moaned against Mal'ik's mouth as he rutted against him, unabashedly pleasuring himself on Mal'ik. Mal'ik's fingers dug into Oliver's hips as he urged Oliver on. Then he shook his head and nipped at Oliver's lips.

"No, I know how I want to finish you, Oliver." Mal'ik grabbed him around the ribs, his metal fingers digging in but not breaking the skin. He walked him backward and then tossed him onto the bed.

Oliver laughed as he bounced, delight sparking through him. It was *fun* to be with Mal'ik. Pleasurable and open and light. Oliver had practically forgotten there was even such a feeling as fun. He looked at Mal'ik still standing at the foot of the bed, grinning at him.

Oliver grinned back and then twisted and arched to show off his body, luxuriating in the way Mal'ik's eyes darkened. He trailed his own gaze obviously down his muscular form. "You'd better hurry up then, or I might finish just from looking at you."

Mal'ik threw back his head and laughed and then shook it. "I don't think so."

Mal'ik grabbed the half-empty vial of oil that had been sitting innocuously on the bedside table since last night, and Oliver's heart jumped in anticipation. Before he could spread his legs, Mal'ik grabbed his ankle like he had last time and pulled him down the bed. Oliver let out an absurd little giggle that hiccuped into a moan when Mal'ik grabbed both his knees and spread his thighs. Exposure felt almost as good as invasion.

He looked down his body so he could see Mal'ik's nosing at the crease of his hips and his sac, fluttering little shivers running through him both at the feel and the knowledge that Mal'ik was smelling him. Smelling him and loving it.

Mal'ik's orange eyes flickered up to him as he massaged Oliver's hip. "I just want you to enjoy this, Oliver."

"I—" Oliver licked his lips. "I already am."

Mal'ik smiled softly. "Good."

Then he sucked the head of Oliver's cock into the warm heat of his mouth. Oliver dropped back onto the bed with a low, drawn-out sigh and let the bliss course through him. He tangled one hand into his own hair and reached down to grasp at Mal'ik's. A pleased growl vibrated up Oliver's length when he managed to tangle his fingers in Mal'ik's locks, and Oliver gasped at the sensation.

"Mal'ik, Mal'ik," Oliver whispered his name over and over again as the sweet sensations mounted. Mal'ik took his time, first rolling his tongue over and around Oliver's sensitive head and then slowly dipping down to wrap his lips around his shaft. Wave after wave of pleasure pulsed through Oliver, never threatening to crest, just wringing out every last ounce of tension until he was a puddle on the bed.

Mal'ik bobbed back up to suckle on the tip of Oliver's length, then circled his entrance with an oiled finger.

"Yes." Oliver nodded and twitched his hips clumsily. "Yes, do it, p—oh yes."

Mal'ik slid his finger in easily, Oliver's hole already loose and relaxed from the nonstop bliss running through him. Oliver rolled his head back and forth, pulled on Mal'ik's hair, and moaned. It was perfect. It was all perfect. Pleasure, happiness, warmth—

Oliver cried out as Mal'ik touched the spot inside him that sent lightning up his spine.

Mal'ik pulled off him long enough to let out a low laugh. "That's what I wanted."

He pushed a second finger past Oliver's rim, then crooked them both, and Oliver arched off the bed.

"Mal'ik!" Oliver's yelp dissolved into a keen as Mal'ik did it again and then increased his pace.

"There you go." Mal'ik pushed himself from the floor to hover over Oliver, staring down at him as he worked inside him. He planted his metal arm on the mattress, leaving Oliver free to writhe on the bed untouched except where he was impaled on Mal'ik's fingers.

Oliver couldn't form words, the sensations over-whelming him as Mal'ik assaulted that spot, sending him higher and higher. He sobbed and reached out to wrap his arms around Mal'ik's neck, needing to anchor himself before he was swept away.

"I've got you." Mal'ik kissed his ear. "Are you going to come? Are you ready?"

Oliver nodded desperately, unable to say the words

around his own moans. He was so ready; he needed it so bad it hurt.

"I've got you." Mal'ik ducked out from under the circle of Oliver's arms and swallowed Oliver's cock again, all the way down to his base.

Oliver seized up as the suction of Mal'ik's throat tightened around him and Mal'ik ground his fingers into that spot. His vision burst into stars as he came, hips stuttering, his release pumping into Mal'ik's mouth. Mal'ik held Oliver's hips down as they jerked with his cold metal fingers and kept his lips sealed around the base of Oliver's cock.

Still floating down, Oliver moaned lightly at the feel of Mal'ik swallowing around him, and then when he pulled off, the soft swipes of his tongue up his shaft and around his crown. He shivered with oversensitivity when Mal'ik pressed one last kiss under his head.

"You're clean." Mal'ik crawled up his sated body and smiled down at him.

Oliver's lips parted as he realized what Mal'ik had done. He glanced down his body to see the faint glisten of saliva and oil but not a drop of semen. He looked back up at Mal'ik, his heart in his throat.

Mal'ik smiled crookedly. "Almost."

Mal'ik took off his own shirt and, before Oliver could protest, wiped away the bit of slickness still between Oliver's legs. Oliver's limbs felt too heavy to struggle, and it felt too good to bother.

Mal'ik shrugged. "I'm about to change anyway."

Oliver reached for him drowsily. "Mal'ik."

He pulled the big man down for a soft kiss that tasted like himself, and Mal'ik hummed and reached up to run his calloused thumb over Oliver's jaw. Oliver's eyes closed, emotional exhaustion and post-orgasmic bliss taking their toll. Oliver felt the covers beneath him start to bunch under his back, and he broke the kiss to see Mal'ik pulling the covers down. He laughed as Mal'ik yanked them down and then rolled Oliver onto the sheets.

"What are you doing?"

Mal'ik kissed his forehead. "Putting you to bed."

"But what about you?" Oliver frowned and tried to reach down to Mal'ik's hips, but Mal'ik batted his hands away.

"Shh, don't worry about me." Mal'ik pulled the covers up to his chin, and Oliver had to concede that he was too tired to argue. Already his eyes were fighting to close. "Go to sleep."

"Mal'ik." Oliver's sleepy mind couldn't think what to say, so he just sighed and settled into the pillows. "Good night."

"Good night, Oliver."

OLIVER SLOWLY WOKE the next morning, his limbs loose and heavy. He scrubbed his hand over his face and was almost baffled to feel a sleepy smile on his lips. Was this how normal people felt after a night with someone?

He rolled over and looked at his empty bed. Well, part of a night with someone. He should ask Mal'ik to stay next time. How much more amazing would it feel to wake up beside Mal'ik's warm bulk?

He bet Mal'ik would kiss him in the mornings before they got up, casual and drowsy. He seemed like the sort.

A cold shiver of fear shot down Oliver's spine, and he shook himself. What was he thinking? There were not going to be sleepy mornings with Mal'ik. For one, he didn't even know if Mal'ik wanted that, and for another, their arrangement was temporary.

He had absolutely no reason to believe that there was a long-term future with Mal'ik, and it was terrifying that he was allowing himself to so concretely fantasize about one.

Well, no reason except for the way that Mal'ik touched him, kissed him, checked on him, listened to him, and smiled at him. And the way that whenever he looked at him, Oliver's heart filled up like the hot-air balloon his father had once taken him and Dominic on when they were very little.

Oliver forced himself out of bed and to get ready to face the day because he was sure it would be a long one.

It was.

After the brief moment of hot-air balloon as Mal'ik arrived to fetch him with that aforementioned soft smile— but no kisses, it was business hours after all—the day was an endless exercise in frustration and futility.

Emissary Serihk seemed to have gotten to everyone. Everyone suddenly wanted to rehash every demand and request and required endless justification, reasoning, and evidence. Even the education minister—for whom Oliver was securing the largest education budget a Klah'Eel planet had ever seen—was pushing back.

And the frustration wasn't that Oliver didn't have watertight arguments for everything—he did—it was that he had already given those arguments. He had already persuaded these people. And now they were having second thoughts, all because Serihk was sowing doubts in their minds about Oliver's intentions.

Oliver's plans were solid, well-reasoned and well-researched, but they were radical and expensive. And it was true that his real mission here was to further enrich the Turner family. So it didn't take much to sour people to his way of thinking. His general demeanor and personality surely didn't help.

He had never persuaded people by making friends. He persuaded them by assuring them that he was the smartest and most powerful person in the room. That fell apart when Serihk was in the room as well.

Oliver would need to swallow his pride and talk to the man again in person. Privately. There was no reason they should be at odds, not politically, at least. Emissary Serihk wanted stability so he could solve the refugee crisis. Oliver wanted stability so he could build factories and rise to the top of the Turner family. Their desired results dovetailed perfectly; they should be partners, not enemies.

Oliver was fuming and nursing an anger headache by late that afternoon, sitting in a lounge with a cup of coffee —not that terrible klak other species seemed to prefer. Mal'ik was on the other side of the room, bent over a data tablet with the human on his team. The man was older but handsome, with streaks of gray running through his dark hair and the stubble on his jaw. He was the right age to have been in the war, and Oliver wondered which side he had fought for.

The whole day might have been more tolerable if he'd been able to bitch and moan to Mal'ik between meetings, but the man was clearly busy. He had been muttering into his earpiece all day, and this was the third time the human had come to speak to him in person. A young klah'eel woman with long black braids made frequent appearances as well, and Mal'ik's brows were always more deeply furrowed when she left.

It had taken Oliver most of the morning to realize that the slight clinking sound he kept hearing when he stood close to Mal'ik was the sound of him tapping his metal thumb and middle finger together. A fidget.

The human put his data tablet away, nodded at Mal'ik, and left, and then Mal'ik finally approached Oliver.

"What's going on?" Oliver asked, more to make conversation with Mal'ik and give his brain a break from politics than because he was worried. There were always security threats when powerful people gathered in one place. That's why they had security.

"Nothing to worry about." Mal'ik shook his head, and Oliver wasn't surprised. Security personnel never wanted to tell their charges anything. People could get panicky and annoying.

"Who's the human on your team?"

"Patrick Smith. You can trust him."

"I didn't say I didn't." Oliver shrugged. "He's Klah'Eel?"

"Yes."

Oliver opened his mouth to say more, but then Mal'ik put his hand to his ear and cocked his head in a way that meant someone was speaking to him, and he turned away from Oliver again. So Oliver shut his mouth with a sigh and downed the rest of his coffee.

A long day indeed.

And a lonely night. Mal'ik came in at the end of the evening to tell him that he would be away for most of the night, dealing with security concerns. Insecurity had risen sharply in Oliver's chest—surely Mal'ik just didn't want to stay with him and he was being kind—but then Mal'ik had kissed him bruisingly, once, twice, three times before finally pulling away.

And then he had kissed his forehead again just before opening the door, and Oliver had seen the sincerity in his eyes. And he felt silly. Mal'ik might not always want him, but he certainly wanted him now, and he certainly wasn't a liar.

So Oliver had gone to bed. Disappointed. And lonely. But not as lonely.

DOMINIC *and I will be on Carta in two days.*

Oliver stared at the message from his father and pinched the bridge of his nose. He hadn't even gotten out of bed yet, and already the headache was forming. Alistair Turner was a master of layering meaning into terse sentences.

Carta was barely a stone's throw from Tava, so, *Dominic and I will be on Carta in two days* actually meant *I've heard that you're running into issues on Tava and that your plans are starting to fall apart. You had better not fuck it up and make me regret giving you this chance. Dominic is here with me because he's actually useful and responsible, and I probably don't need you anymore at all. I'm coming to watch over you, and I'll swoop in if I think I have to. You have two days.*

Oliver dropped his head back onto his pillow with a sigh.

And then from his brother: *I'll see you soon, little brother. I'm very busy, but maybe we'll have a chance to catch up.*

Which was more bullshit. It was just Dominic making sure he knew how much work their father had entrusted to him and not Oliver.

Oliver let out a little growl and then rolled out of bed. Two days was more than enough time. All he needed was to get Emissary Serihk on his side. The Klah'Eel ministers were easily swayed by the strongest person in the room, so he was done spending his time on them. He already had a meeting with the qesh scheduled for late morning. He'd have a bow on everything in a day and a half.

A hot shower later, his headache was gone, and he was feeling confident again. He was just opening his wardrobe to choose something that said 'competent but conciliatory and maybe even compassionate' when he heard the familiar heavy knock on his door and Mal'ik's voice.

"Turner, I'm coming in."

Maybe whatever had been concerning Mal'ik yesterday had been resolved and Oliver could go back to chattering at him. He padded into the foyer with a soft white towel wrapped around his waist and then pulled up short.

Mal'ik wasn't alone. The human man—Patrick Smith —stood beside him, and the man's eyebrows rose at the sight of Oliver nearly naked in the doorway. Oliver felt heat on the back of his neck and was thankful only Mal'ik would be able to smell his embarrassment. He kept his face neutral, as though he greeted all of his bodyguards in a towel in the morning.

"Well, good morning," he managed in a smooth voice. "I don't think we've been introduced."

"No, we haven't." Smith did not manage his voice so well. It was a little bit high, and he had splotches of red on his cheeks. "Patrick Smith. I'll be joining your close protection team with Captain Mal'ik for the next few days."

Oliver frowned.

Word must have spread of what he and Mal'ik had done. They hadn't exactly been quiet, and guards had been posted just outside. Guards with a klah'eel's sense of smell. Was Smith here because they were worried Mal'ik had been compromised?

"Oliver Turner. A pleasure to meet you." He smiled his fake professional smile at Smith and then looked at Mal'ik. "Captain Mal'ik, may I speak with you alone for a moment?"

Mal'ik nodded and followed him into the bedroom. Oliver shut the door behind them. "Why is he here?" he demanded in a whisper.

"There are some security concerns that a larger team

exacerbates." Mal'ik tilted his head toward Oliver and matched his quiet tone. "I'm shrinking the team for a few days and bringing it closer. I've chosen Patrick because I know him better than I know anyone in the world. I trust him with my life and yours."

Oliver's eyes widened. Those were heavy words. He wanted to dig more into the relationship between Mal'ik and Patrick, but he didn't.

"So then it's not because…" Oliver grimaced as he found himself forced to put words to whatever they were. "Because of what we're doing?"

"No, Oliver." Mal'ik smiled softly, and Oliver had the impression he would touch his cheek had it been after the workday instead of before. "It's not about that at all."

Oliver nodded tersely and turned away before he gave in to the desire to reach out and touch Mal'ik. He was so close, and Oliver could feel the warmth of his body and the masculine smell of him. But he had an important day ahead—the most important day of his life maybe—and he couldn't be distracted.

So Oliver went back to his wardrobe and opened it up. In the moment before he dropped his towel to dress, he heard the door open and close and looked over his shoulder to see that Mal'ik had left him. Had given him privacy, Oliver corrected himself.

In a few minutes, Oliver was ready. He rolled his neck, shrugged on the emotional armor of Oliver Turner, representative of the Turner family, and strode back out into the foyer. Patrick and Mal'ik had their heads together again and glanced up when he entered. Patrick didn't react to the sight of him, but Mal'ik's orange eyes flickered over Oliver's body and he stood up a little straighter.

"Shall we?" Oliver gestured to the door behind them.

"We shall." Patrick nodded with a smile that made his grizzled face look boyish and then exited the room first.

The first hour or so of the new arrangement was awkward and silent. Oliver felt strangely self-conscious with both Patrick and Mal'ik flanking him. Patrick was Mal'ik's oldest friend from the sound of it. And he must know about what they were doing. What if he found Oliver wanting? What if he didn't think Oliver was good enough for Mal'ik? What if he thought Oliver was a prissy bastard and told Mal'ik so? Not that Oliver wasn't or that Mal'ik didn't already know....

But after his first meeting—with the minister of the military who Oliver had back on his side in moments, nodding along as though he couldn't possibly disagree with Oliver's points—he was feeling more like himself. Enough like himself to scoff at the wilted flowers lining the arcade. Patrick snorted with that boyish smile, and Mal'ik's scarred lips twitched, and Oliver felt settled back into himself.

By the time they were approaching Emissary Serihk's ship—Oliver had agreed to meet there once again in his bid to win the qesh's favor—he was feeling as confident as ever.

It opened before they reached the door, and a young human girl stepped out. She had a gatlung slung over her shoulder that rivaled her in height, and when she caught sight of them, her eyes lit up. Oliver stopped, taken aback.

"Captain Mal'ik!" She grinned and trotted down the gangway to meet them. "Look what I have." She pulled her gatlung off her shoulder and spun it impressively. Oliver fought the urge to step back when that serrated blade swept disconcertingly close to him.

"You're very first. May it serve you well," Mal'ik replied in that warm rumble and smiled. The sight of him smiling as a human child bounced around him made Oliver's heart ache. "I'm surprised you're still here."

"I leave in two days." The girl shifted and swallowed, but she still looked excited.

"Good luck," Mal'ik said.

"Thanks." She grinned at him, then pulled the gatlung back over her shoulder. "Anyway, I have to go. Lar'a found an old friend to give me lessons today."

"Well, good luck twice then."

The girl bounced off, and Oliver raised an eyebrow at Mal'ik.

"Astrid Harrison," Mal'ik replied. "Bryant Harrison's daughter."

"He has a daughter?" Oliver frowned. He had tried to dig up everything he could after he'd found out about Serihk's human consultant, but it was like the man had suddenly appeared out of nowhere. Serihk had gone to Lewis Station alone, and when he'd come back, he was carting some human consultant along with him everywhere.

Some human consultant with an uneducated accent, a very rough exterior, and apparently a daughter. Oliver had disliked him immediately on principle—he clearly hadn't thought much of Oliver and had the gall to stand opposite him. The shrewd look in his eye as he'd sat through the humiliating and torturous meeting hadn't endeared Oliver to him either.

But of course Mal'ik would be friends with his daughter. The stoic bodyguard seemed to have the knack for making friends that Oliver never had.

Oliver turned back to the ship to see Bryant Harrison himself standing in the entryway, watching them. Oliver schooled his expression into something polite, even friendly.

"Good morning, Mr. Harrison." Oliver smiled as he walked up the gangway toward him and reached out his hand. Harrison's eyebrows went up at the gesture, but he took it and gave Oliver a firm handshake.

"Good morning, Mr. Turner." Then he reached past Oliver to Mal'ik. "Captain Mal'ik. Good to see you again."

"And you, Harrison." Mal'ik shook his hand, and Oliver stepped aside. Right, Mal'ik had been here just the other night. Friends with everyone. "This is Patrick Smith. He's on the security team."

"Pleasure to meet you." Patrick shook Harrison's hand.

"Serihk's in the study." Harrison nodded down the hall, and they followed. Apparently, Oliver's bodyguards were accompanying him this time with or without his explicit consent. Oliver found that strangely comforting, though he'd never admit it.

But a klah'eel woman stood outside the study door, and as soon as she saw them, she pointed at Mal'ik and Patrick.

"You two. I need to speak to you." Her voice didn't leave a lot of room for argument, but even so, Oliver glanced at Mal'ik to see him hesitating. Mal'ik glanced down at Oliver—their eyes met—then back at the woman. The woman scowled. "It's urgent."

Finally, Mal'ik relented. "Alright." He looked back down at Oliver, and when he spoke, his voice was comforting. "I'll be in soon."

Oliver became hyperaware of the number of eyes on them and put his back up. The last thing he wanted was for everyone to think he needed his bodyguard to babysit him through meetings, so he turned to the door and waved his hand dismissively over his shoulder.

"Do whatever you need to," he said, then brushed past Harrison into the study.

Emissary Serihk was sitting at his desk, looking at a

data tablet, and he glanced up when Oliver entered. As though he had forgotten Oliver was coming and was still trying to get some work done. As though Oliver had made an appointment with him rather than organized a meeting of equals.

Oliver inhaled deeply and let it out quietly. Serihk was trying to make him indignant. He was trying to offend because he knew Oliver would react poorly. So Oliver wouldn't.

Instead, he smiled and sat in the chair across from Serihk without being invited. "Good morning, Serihk. How are you?"

Serihk raised an eyebrow and set the tablet aside. He laced his long fingers together and leaned forward. "Good morning. I'm well. And you?"

"I'm feeling like we got off to a bad start." Oliver leaned forward to mirror him. His usual instincts were to lean back, make distance, and lord over whomever he was speaking to, but he fought them. When he heard Harrison enter, Oliver shot him as genuine a smile as he could manage.

Serihk's lips quirked up. "Is that so?"

"I think we want the same things."

Oliver jerked back when Serihk barked out a laugh. The qesh untangled his hands and pressed his palms onto the surface of his desk. He stood up and loomed over Oliver, green stripes beginning to ripple up his throat. "I don't. I think you want to exploit Southern Tava and everyone in it to enrich yourself and your family, and if you have to take control of the local government and undermine democracy and the rule of law to do it, then you will."

Oliver pushed himself from his chair and opened his mouth to snap back but paused when Harrison stepped forward and placed a big hand on Serihk's shoulder. He watched on in surprise as Serihk's aggressive posture loosened and the green receded back below his collar. Then Harrison shot Oliver a stern but calm look.

"Both of you sit back down," he said in his low voice with those rounded vowels. Serihk dropped back into his seat, and Oliver slowly descended as well until they were once again seated at the desk like civilized people.

Oliver took a breath and proceeded calmly, "There is nothing in my proposals that undermines democracy or the rule of law."

"You are an unelected body attempting to control the running of a democratic state."

"Through agreements with the properly elected officials." Oliver raised a finger. "Officials whom the people have chosen to make agreements on their behalf."

"Governor Tesh seems to feel you're less making agreements and more making threats and bribes." Serihk leaned back and lifted his chin challengingly.

He dropped it, though, when Harrison spoke from beside him. "I'd be more worried why this Governor Tesh feels threatened by money for education and healthcare."

Oliver's mouth dropped open in surprise at his sudden ally, but he jumped on the opportunity quickly. "Yes, exactly. His position isn't in any way diminished by my proposals, quite the opposite."

Serihk frowned. "Other than that you'll own him."

"I will not. My family will simply have a seat at the governing table."

"A very large seat," Harrison added, and Oliver shot him a look. Whose side was he on?

"Fine, yes," Oliver agreed. "We will have a lot of power, but what Southern Tava gets in exchange is stability, jobs, infrastructure."

Serihk scoffed. "Peace and prosperity? Is that right?"

"Yes, it is." Oliver scowled. "You want to solve the refugee crisis in the surrounding system, I want to go home with a win for my family. We can find a compromise here, Emissary Serihk."

"It was my terrible compromise that got us into this mess in the first place," Serihk barked, red and orange flooding up his throat. "I won't make the same mistake twice."

Oliver gaped at him, and even Harrison stared before setting a hand on Serihk's forearm. "Serihk—"

The door slid open with a hiss. Mal'ik and Patrick swept into the room, footsteps heavy on the soft carpet, with the klah'eel woman on their heels.

Mal'ik reached Oliver first and grabbed his upper arm with more force than he had that day in the courtyard when his scent cream had dripped off. "We need to go. Now."

A familiar feeling of alarm shot up Oliver's spine, and he obediently jumped to his feet. Bodyguards had been grabbing at him and telling him to move fast his entire life. He'd learned quickly when it was time to listen.

Serihk was also moving, on his feet and meeting the klah'eel woman halfway across the room. "What's happening?"

"We need to get off the ship." She grabbed him like Mal'ik had grabbed Oliver and then barked at Harrison. "Bryant, now!"

She dragged the qesh out into the hall, Harrison on her heels and Patrick and Mal'ik frog-marching Oliver after them. Oliver's heart pounded in his chest. His breath came in short gasps, and he realized distantly that he was panicking. Which made him panic more because he knew how dangerous it was to panic.

He reached blindly for where Mal'ik was beside him and found the metal wrist of the hand holding his arm. He wrapped his fingers around it and held on, letting the cool metal ground him as they hurried to the exit.

"Mal'ik," he managed out through clenched teeth as they got to the door and crested the ramp to the gangway.

Mal'ik squeezed his arm. "I'll explain in a moment. Don't—"

The ship exploded out from under them.

Chapter Six

OLIVER'S FEET left the ground. His arm ripped from Mal'ik's grasp. He flew through the air, his ears ringing, his vision blurring. His stomach dropped out from his belly, and he scrambled and thrashed at nothing.

Then he hit the ground.

His breath left his body, but he didn't black out.

He lay on the concrete, staring through the smoke and dust and the stars behind his own eyes at the hangar ceiling, gasping and gulping air into his lungs. A dark shape suddenly obscured his view, and he tried to yell and twist away, but a heavy hand dropped onto his shoulder.

"Oliver. It's me. It's Patrick. I've got you."

Oliver stopped twisting as conscious thought retook hold of his brain. He scrambled up to sit, and Patrick let him go.

Oliver blinked a few times to clear his vision and saw Patrick's broad back in front of him. The man stood in a low stance with his gatlung out and his head on a swivel. Black smoke billowed up from the hole where the front half of the ship had been, filling up the top of the hangar, and dust still eddied in the air. Large bits of debris lay scattered all around them. Oliver pushed to his feet, looking frantically for other people.

His eyes honed in on a large shape rushing toward them. Overwhelming relief flooded through his system. "Mal'ik!"

He started to run toward the klah'eel, but Patrick's hand clamped down on his arm like a vice. "Wait."

"What? Why?" Oliver twisted to look at Patrick, who ignored him to stare ahead at Mal'ik. Cold fear slipped into Oliver's heart at the narrow, calculating look in Patrick's eye. He tried to pull his arm back. "Let go."

Instead, Patrick tightened his grip to bruising and yanked Oliver behind him. He swung his gatlung out to face Mal'ik. "That's close enough."

Mal'ik swung his own gatlung into his hand and kept striding toward them. "Let him go."

"That's close enough!"

Mal'ik snarled. "Let him go!"

"Stop, Mal'ik!" Desperation rang in Patrick's voice.

Mal'ik halted.

They stared at each other from just out of range.

"What are you doing?" Oliver demanded, eyes snapping from one to the other. They both looked ready to kill. "Mal'ik—"

"Just hold on a second," Patrick snapped, turning his head toward Oliver but keeping his eyes trained on Mal'ik. He licked his lips and grit his teeth, and Oliver saw his knuckles whiten on the handle of his weapon. "You know there's nothing I can do here. I won't put down my weapon."

Mal'ik's shoulders fell. "You're right." He tossed his gatlung out of reach, and it hit the ground with a loud clatter. Oliver gaped as Mal'ik dropped to his knees and then dropped his chin down to his chest. "Check me."

Patrick let Oliver go and started toward Mal'ik.

"Don't hurt him!" Oliver grabbed Patrick without thinking and yanked him back. He didn't know what was happening, but he knew if he had to choose someone to trust, it was Mal'ik and not this man. Oliver wasn't going to sit back and watch as he brought that nasty blade anywhere near Mal'ik.

"What—"

"Don't fucking touch him." Oliver grabbed Patrick's armored vest and pulled and yanked, forcing himself between him and Mal'ik. Patrick tried to shove him off, but Oliver just grabbed the wrist of the arm he tried to shove him with and held on tight.

"Oliver!" Mal'ik's deep voice and urgent tone cut through Oliver's fight instinct, and Oliver froze, still white-knuckling Patrick's wrist. "It's okay. Let him go."

Oliver tightened his grip and stared at Mal'ik still kneeling on the ground. He stared into those orange eyes, and they seemed confident. Confident enough for Oliver to slowly release Patrick's arm back to him. Just as he let it go, though, he glared back up at Patrick and bared his teeth.

"I'll fucking kill you if you hurt him," he growled.

Patrick looked at him with dark, narrowed eyes. "I won't."

Oliver had no idea how he would kill Patrick if he had to. He had no training and no weapons, and Patrick had both in spades. But as he watched Patrick advance on Mal'ik kneeling on the ground with his neck exposed, Oliver was pretty sure he could fucking find a way.

Patrick got to Mal'ik and shoved Mal'ik's dark hair to the side with his free hand. He ran it up and down the back of Mal'ik's neck and behind his ears. Then he let out a sigh of relief, and his posture dropped. Oliver hadn't realized how tense the man had been. "Clear."

Mal'ik surged up and grabbed Patrick's jaw. Oliver's heart clenched, but Patrick didn't move. He just let Mal'ik turn his head and run his hands over the back of Patrick's neck just like Patrick had done to him.

"Clear." Then Mal'ik turned to Oliver, and Oliver almost ran to him, except the threatening look in his eyes stopped him dead. He took a step back.

"Mal'ik? What are you doing?"

"Come here, Oliver," Mal'ik ordered. Oliver couldn't make himself take a step toward him, but he forced himself to stop taking any steps back. He stood, frozen, as Mal'ik got to him and grabbed his jaw just like he'd grabbed Patrick's.

His grip was gentler, though, his fingers soft as they traced over the back of his neck and the hollows behind his ears. It would feel nice if they weren't standing in the middle of the wreckage of an explosion and if Mal'ik didn't seem like he was still ready for a fight—possibly with Oliver.

But then Mal'ik wrapped his arms around Oliver and pulled him into his chest, and it was definitely a hug and not an attack. "Clear."

Oliver let himself collapse into Mal'ik's solid weight. The fear and tension that had been building to a fever pitch inside him drained out. He didn't know what Patrick and Mal'ik had been afraid of, but whatever it was, that danger seemed to have passed.

"They found another one, Mal'ik," Patrick said from behind him, voice calm but urgent. "We need to get moving."

"Let's take him to my rooms." Mal'ik let Oliver go and turned to Patrick. "Back way. Try not to be seen."

Patrick nodded and led the way to the back of the hangar. Mal'ik put a hand between Oliver's shoulder blades and pushed him to follow, bringing up the rear just at Oliver's back.

"Another bomb?" Oliver asked.

"No." Patrick shook his head. "Another body. A servant not far from here."

"A body?" Oliver repeated. "What does that have to do with anything?" He glanced back at Mal'ik, but Mal'ik wasn't looking at him, too busy scanning behind them, in front of them, and all around.

Patrick got to the hangar exit and held out a hand to stop Oliver. He peeked his head out into the hallway, looking both ways, and then beckoned for them to keep moving.

"They had cuts in the backs of their necks." Patrick tapped his forefinger over his own spinal vertebrae. "A torvar's cuts."

Oliver froze in shock, only to be kept moving when Mal'ik gave him another shove between the shoulder blades.

"A torvar? Those are…" Oliver was about to say real, but of course, he knew they were real. They were a recognized species. Oliver had just so rarely heard of them. And he had never wanted to. "Here?"

"There are a number of them in Southern Tava." Patrick looked around the corner of the next hall they got to, then waved them toward the left. Oliver didn't know where they were going, but it didn't seem to be back to their old rooms. "Impossible to know how many, obviously."

"You never know who the worms might be hiding in," Mal'ik growled from behind Oliver.

"They've always been peaceful enough." Patrick shot a

look over his shoulder at Mal'ik. "They're not body snatchers."

Mal'ik lifted his upper lip in a look of disgust Oliver had never seen on his face before. "Aren't they?"

Oliver had the impression he was witnessing an old argument and cut in. "Well, this one obviously isn't peaceful. Where did it come from?"

"The Resistance," Patrick replied. "No idea how it got in, though. Stay here while I check these next two rooms."

Oliver and Mal'ik stopped while Patrick went on ahead. Mal'ik stood close enough behind Oliver for Oliver to feel the heat of him. "We got word that the Resistance had a torvar in their ranks. We've been checking all personnel. No one's been allowed in without submitting to a search."

"Except for participants in the talks." Oliver grimaced. He hadn't been checked, and he would have remembered if someone had breathed of a torvar threat. He glanced up at Mal'ik to see a matching frown on his face. They had a traitor. And a high-up one.

Just then, Patrick came striding back toward them. "Alright, we—"

A deep boom sounded, close enough to shake the ground under them but far enough not to threaten them directly.

"That was the direction of the main meeting rooms," Mal'ik said.

Patrick nodded and spun on his heel. "Yeah. We gotta go." He put his hand to his ear. "Report."

The three of them picked up their pace, winding through hallways and arcades and around buildings, into a part of the complex Oliver had never been to. Patrick and Mal'ik barked orders and questions into their mouthpieces.

Two more explosions in quick succession rocked the

area, and Patrick came to a sudden stop in front of them. "You're sure? You're absolutely sure? Fucking chase him then! And tell everyone else to be on the lookout."

"Go," Mal'ik ordered. He came up behind Oliver and put his hand on Oliver's shoulder. Oliver jumped when he felt skin against his and looked down to see that his clothes were torn, bloody from scrapes and scratches that he was only now starting to feel. Dirt and dust coated him, and Mal'ik's hand on his shoulder mixed it with his own sweat and turned it into a grime.

Oliver shuddered and pulled away.

Mal'ik glanced at him briefly and dropped his hand, then jutted his chin at Patrick. "Go. Help them. I'll get him to safety."

Patrick nodded sharply and took off at a run in the direction of the last explosion.

Mal'ik didn't grab Oliver again, just nudged his shoulder as he passed. "Follow me."

They moved faster without Patrick scouting ahead, but they passed more people, mostly klah'eel, some rushing this way and that, and some standing and gaping at the columns of billowing black smoke rising into the air.

They got to a large building with many doors in a few minutes. It looked like a barracks or housing complex of some kind, and Mal'ik led Oliver to a room on the first floor in the middle of the building. Mal'ik glanced quickly over both his shoulders, then input the door codes. He grabbed Oliver's wrist, pulled him inside, and shut the door behind him.

It wasn't until the door slid closed that Oliver realized how loud it had been out there. Alarms, sirens, people yelling and screaming, the ringing of his own ears, and the sound of their pounding footsteps. The door sealed it all away, and everything suddenly felt still and quiet.

It made Oliver's own ragged breath seem very loud and gave his mind a chance to fall back to what had just happened.

The ground ripping out from under his feet.

Falling through the air.

The high-pitched ring in his ears and the inability to breathe.

Being crushed by stone—no. Oliver shook his head. No, that hadn't been this time. He knelt down on the ground as his knees shook. He pressed his palm to the carpeted floor, feeling the solidity of it beneath him.

"Hey, Oliver." Mal'ik's voice came to him slowly through the air as though it were water. Oliver looked up to see Mal'ik crouched in front of him. Mal'ik reached out a hand and touched his jaw with the pads of his fingers. It emphasized the grit covering his skin, and Oliver cringed.

"I need a shower." Oliver gulped and pushed himself up to his feet. He swayed but didn't fall. "I need to be clean."

"This way." Mal'ik didn't question him, just turned and led him deeper into the rooms. Oliver didn't see his surroundings. He just focused on Mal'ik's broad shoulders and keeping his breath whooshing steadily in and out of his chest.

He heard the sound of water flowing from a shower-head just before he stepped into the bathroom. Mal'ik pulled the shower door open for him, then gestured to a towel on the toilet's lid.

"I'll be just outside, alright?" Mal'ik stepped forward to look into Oliver's eyes.

Oliver met them and nodded. "Alright."

Oliver didn't wait to see Mal'ik leave. He stripped off his ruined clothes, stepped into the lukewarm spray of the shower, and closed his eyes.

MAL'IK DIDN'T CLOSE the bathroom door all the way. He didn't think Oliver would collapse or have a breakdown, but he wanted to hear if he did, so he left it cracked.

Patrick had cut comms a few minutes ago—worried the torvar might have wriggled into one of their team members' bodies—and so now Mal'ik could do nothing but wait. He hadn't heard any more explosions, but he wasn't assuming the all clear until Patrick himself arrived to tell him so.

He hoped Lar'a had gotten herself, Serihk, and Bryant out. He hadn't seen her since she'd been hurrying down the gangway right before it was blown to smithereens.

Along with Oliver. Mal'ik let out a shuddering breath. Nearly. *Nearly* along with Oliver. Mal'ik looked back at the bathroom to see steam falling through the crack of the door.

He was fine.

Physically, at least. Mal'ik had seen nothing more than a few scratches on the surface, and he hadn't moved like someone with internal injuries. And he didn't smell like blood. Just fear, with a few whiffs of quickly controlled panic.

He had practice managing his own terror, Mal'ik realized, and the thought made his heart ache. He fought the urge to go into the bathroom and be near him. Oliver needed Mal'ik to protect him right now, not coo over him. Mal'ik's comfort would be of little use if the torvar found them vulnerable here.

So he sat on a chair in the bedroom, alert and rubbing at the skin that itched and ached where his stump met his prosthetic.

After a few more minutes, there was a quiet knock on

the front door. Mal'ik glanced at the door to the bathroom where he could still hear the shower, then crept into the living room. He peered through the door's viewer.

Patrick.

Ostensibly.

"Get on your knees and move your weapons out of reach," Mal'ik demanded through the heavy wood. Patrick did as he was told and dropped his chin to expose his neck. Mal'ik quickly opened the door and checked him. "Clear." Mal'ik pulled him into the room and shut the door. "What's the news?"

"We got him." Patrick's lip was split and oozing blood, and he was covered in debris, but other than that, he looked fine. He collapsed against the closed door and rubbed his eyes with his palms. "He's in a holding cell. I've warned and triple-warned everyone not to get into the same room with him. So, hopefully, he'll stay there."

"Who's he wearing?" Mal'ik crossed his arms.

Patrick grimaced. "Governor Tesh."

Mal'ik matched his grimace. "Was Tesh in the wrong place at the wrong time?"

"Or was he a dirty traitor?" Patrick finished for him. He shrugged. "My money's on dirty traitor based on the caliber of encryption on his data tablet. But we're still trying to break it, so we'll see."

Mal'ik nodded slowly, letting that sit on him before letting it slide off. Politics were other people's problems. Someone else would have to figure out what to do with a traitor. "Is it over then? Or do we have other concerns?"

"There's been a lot of destruction." Patrick smelled exhausted, stressed, mournful. It had been a long time since Mal'ik had smelled that combination on him, and Mal'ik clasped his hand on Patrick's shoulder as he went on. "Rescue efforts are under way, but there could be more bombs hidden, either on timers or other triggers."

"I'll keep Oliver here for a while longer then."

Patrick nodded. "Yeah. There's another thing."

Mal'ik's stomach went cold, but he spoke evenly. "Tell me."

"They took out our communication towers first. We still haven't had any contact with anyone outside."

Mal'ik tilted his head and narrowed his eyes. "That's not surprising." It was quite a standard tactic for the Resistance. "What's bothering you?"

"I'm not sure." Patrick shook his head. "I just have a bad feeling." He straightened and shook his head again, this time as if he were tossing the thoughts out of it like water. "I should get going. I'll come back when we've finished sweeping all the buildings."

"Any word on Lar'a?" Mal'ik asked before he left.

"No." Only the barest thread of tightness in Patrick's voice gave away his worry. "She's either buried in the hangar, or she's gone to ground with her two men just like you have."

Mal'ik nodded. "Alright. Send me all the information on the attack as it's gathered. I want to know everything."

"Of course."

"Be safe."

Mal'ik closed and locked the door behind him. He stood there for a few seconds, breathing deeply and letting his mindset shift with the situation. The immediate danger had passed. He could let go of the urgency and the adrenaline. Now was the time for analysis and deciding what to do next.

And for caring for Oliver.

He looked over his shoulder at the bedroom door. The sounds of the shower had stopped. He double-checked the lock on the front door, then walked back to the bedroom. Oliver wasn't in there, and the bathroom door was still mostly closed.

He knocked a single knuckle lightly on the cracked door. "Oliver? Can I come in?"

"Yeah."

Mal'ik pushed the door open to see Oliver standing in front of the mirror, staring into it with his hands braced against the sink as though it was the only thing holding him up. The white towel wrapped around his waist accentuated the paleness of his skin and the angry red of the scrapes, scratches, and contusions along his torso.

Oliver looked up at him from the mirror's reflection as the door swung open. His eyes and forehead were tight, his eyes wide but pinched. "Was that Patrick outside?"

"Yes." Mal'ik didn't dare step any farther into the bathroom, not with the smell he caught drifting off Oliver's clean skin. "They've caught the torvar. It's over, for now."

Oliver hung his head with a heaving sigh. "Thank god." He paused, then turned slowly and leaned back against the sink. He lifted his hazel eyes to Mal'ik's. "Mal'ik."

Mal'ik had to close his eyes against that look and the sweet, earthy molasses scent that rolled off Oliver. His instincts told him to step forward and pull the human against him, but there was fear under that arousal—a lot of fear.

He shook his head slowly as he opened his eyes. "Oliver."

"I'm sorry." Oliver grimaced and glanced away, but then his eyes dragged back to Mal'ik's as though he couldn't help it. "I just...when I thought Patrick might—" He cut himself off with a ragged breath. When Oliver thought Patrick might hurt Mal'ik, Oliver had tried to fight him. The memory of his fierce eyes as he threatened to kill Patrick over Mal'ik made all sorts of emotions Mal'ik couldn't possibly handle swirl in his chest.

"I'm fine," Mal'ik said, and he'd meant to be reassuring, but even he heard the dismissiveness in his tone.

Oliver nodded, and he shrank back a little against the sink, but he couldn't pull back the smell of his own desperation. Oliver bit his lip as he looked up at him. "I'm sorry," he said again. "I'm not trying to be demanding or to put you on the spot. I can go find the scent cream; it might still be in my pocket; I had it in my clothes."

He tried to step past Mal'ik and go back out into the bedroom, but Mal'ik reached out before he could stop himself.

"You don't have to." Mal'ik put a hand on Oliver's arm, stilling him before he got to the door. He didn't grab him, just touched him, but Oliver froze immediately. "I know you hate it."

He'd seen how eager Oliver was to get it off at the end of every day and the flicker of disgust in his eyes as he reapplied it.

Even now, his nose wrinkled. "I do hate it."

Mal'ik huffed a laugh and drew his hand back, but Oliver caught it. The look in his eyes paired with his scent was unmistakable.

"Oliver, you've been through a lot." Mal'ik tried to pull his hand back gently, but Oliver tightened his grip.

"And?"

"And I can smell the fear on you."

"Is that all you can smell?" Oliver stepped in close, so they were chest to chest, just a hairsbreadth of distance between them.

Mal'ik inhaled deeply and growled. "You know it's not."

Oliver's fingers flexed over Mal'ik's wrist. "You can say no, Mal'ik. You can tell me no. Is that what you're doing?"

Mal'ik groaned and shook his head. "I can't say no to you, Oliver."

Mal'ik pulled the loose towel from around Oliver's hips, grabbed the backs of Oliver's thighs, and lifted him into the air. He wrapped Oliver's legs around him, kneaded his hands into the warm bare skin of his ass, and felt him shudder.

"Fuck yes," Oliver hissed as he wrapped his arms around Mal'ik's neck and squirmed against him. He kissed eagerly down the side of Mal'ik's throat and pressed his already hard cock against Mal'ik's abs.

Mal'ik pulled Oliver's hips against him and trapped that hard length against his body. "I'll do anything you want to you."

The smell of fear was gone. Dissipated without a trace. Mal'ik wondered at it for a moment, but then Oliver tugged his earlobe with his teeth, and Mal'ik stopped wondering about anything other than how to get Oliver to writhe with pleasure. He carried Oliver back into the bedroom and tumbled them onto the bed. He settled between Oliver's spread thighs and ran his hands up his lean torso.

Oliver arched up into him. He tangled his fingers into Mal'ik's hair and tugged him toward him. "Kiss me."

Mal'ik went easily, letting Oliver pull him down and slot their mouths together. Oliver's lips were soft—so soft—and his mouth so warm and pliant. When Mal'ik licked at the slit of his lips, he let out a little gasp and surged up to meet him. He thrust his tongue into Mal'ik's mouth and rolled his hips up into him, and Mal'ik moaned into the kiss.

Oliver braced his foot on the mattress and pushed

against him. He was so small compared to Mal'ik. Mal'ik could keep him trapped here if he wanted to, writhing and thrusting and pushing. He entertained the thought for a moment and ran his metal hand up the back of Oliver's thigh to cup the swell of his ass again. But then Oliver whined insistently into his mouth and pushed again, and Mal'ik let himself be rolled onto his back, pulling Oliver over with him to straddle his hips.

Oliver sat up, hair mussed, lips swollen, with color high on his cheeks and his cock standing proudly.

He started pulling at the straps and fastenings of Mal'ik's armor and scowled. "You have so many fucking buckles."

"Well, it's not made to be removed by fussy men in bed." Mal'ik laughed and left off grabbing at every inch of Oliver he could reach and started helping him undo his clothing. Oliver's bit-lip intensity and the eagerness rolling off him made Mal'ik's breath catch in his throat. Oliver wanted *him*, all of him, old scars and metal arm and all. He could have anyone, and he was here on top of Mal'ik, rocking his hips against him and stripping him with insistent, grabby fingers.

It was normal to be aroused after life-threatening situations, Mal'ik reminded himself. He *knew* that. He'd had his fair share of meaningless encounters after close calls. Oliver's desire didn't necessarily mean anything more than that, but the look in Oliver's eyes set something in Mal'ik on fire that had never been lit before.

As soon as Mal'ik's chest was exposed, Oliver groaned. "I can't get over how fucking good you look." He shifted down to drop wet, open-mouthed kisses along Mal'ik's pectorals as Mal'ik's heart clenched behind them. He moved his lips over his muscles and scars and dipped his tongue into the hollow of his collarbone. Then he licked down, down along the lines of his abs.

"Oliver…" Mal'ik propped himself up on his forearms to look down his body. Oliver knelt between his legs and looked up at him with pupils blown wide in his hazel eyes. "What are you doing?"

"I want to suck you." The words tumbled out from between Oliver's lips, and then Oliver clamped them shut again as though he hadn't meant to allow the words to escape. His thumb worried at Mal'ik's belt. He opened his mouth and then shut it again and bit his lip like when he'd first asked Mal'ik to fuck him.

Anxiety, fear, and nervousness oozed out to join the smell of arousal, and something fierce reared up in Mal'ik's chest. He remembered how unprepared Oliver had been that night, how tight around his finger, how nervous and downright inexperienced. And then how pliant and soft he had been the night after. The fussy, astringent man was both sweet and dirty once he was in Mal'ik's bed, and Mal'ik was going to give him everything he wanted.

Mal'ik sat up and cupped Oliver's jaw. He ran his thumb over his soft lower lip and then pulled Oliver's mouth open to press the pad of it down on his tongue.

"Yeah? You want my cock in your pretty mouth, Oliver?"

Oliver moaned and nodded, his eyes locked with Mal'ik. He sealed his lips around Mal'ik's thumb, but before he could suck on it, Mal'ik pulled it out and smeared the spit over his cheekbone. Oliver let out a little gasp as his pupils dilated.

"Get your knees on the ground then," Mal'ik ordered, and Oliver quickly slid off the bed to kneel at the foot of it. Mal'ik stripped his own pants off and moved toward

Oliver to sit at the edge of the bed with his feet braced on the floor and Oliver bracketed between his thighs.

Oliver grabbed Mal'ik's quad muscles with his slender fingers and strained up toward him. "Kiss me again."

Mal'ik was already cupping his neck and bringing their lips together. He could kiss Oliver all night long. He was so eager and responsive, both demanding and yielding. Open and bare in his kisses in a way he never was with his words out of bed. Mal'ik dropped his hand down between them to grab at Oliver's balls just as he pressed his tongue into him, and Oliver gasped and moaned.

Then he tore his mouth away and pushed on Mal'ik's chest. "No, wait. That's not what we're doing."

Mal'ik chuckled and reluctantly pulled his hand back, trailing his fingers up Oliver's velvety cock as they went. "Whatever you say, Oliver."

"I said I want to suck you." Oliver jutted his chin out at him. Still keeping his eyes locked on Mal'ik's face, he wrapped both hands around Mal'ik's cock. Pleasure shot down Mal'ik's spine, and his balls tightened. "And I've been thinking about it for days, so don't distract me now."

Mal'ik's eyes widened. Had he really? Had he really been thinking about touching Mal'ik's body? Not just Mal'ik touching his? But the thoughts were driven out of Mal'ik's mind when Oliver dipped down and sucked the head of Mal'ik's cock into his mouth.

"Oh fuck, Oliver," Mal'ik hissed. He threaded the fingers of both hands into Oliver's blond hair, not pulling or holding, just touching and feeling the way the muscles of his neck and throat clenched as he bobbed.

Oliver moved cautiously at first, short little movements as he suckled at Mal'ik's cockhead. He brought Mal'ik into his hot mouth just deep enough to run his tongue around his crown and to press at the vein on its underside.

Mal'ik smoothed his fingers over Oliver's scalp as his cock gave a pulse of precum. "Good boy, Oliver. That's good." Fuck, Oliver was so inexperienced, and it made every nervous little flick of his tongue along Mal'ik's length feel all that much better.

Oliver made a mewling sound at the praise, and he spread his hands high up on Mal'ik's inner thighs and pushed himself farther onto Mal'ik's cock. Mal'ik groaned as he slid deeper into that wet heat.

"Yes, that's it, Oliver." Mal'ik carded his fingers through Oliver's hair and guided him gently as Oliver pulled back and then sucked Mal'ik back down. "Fuck, yes, that's it, Oliver. Good boy. Just like that."

Mal'ik saw the moment Oliver let go. He saw the tension fall out of his shoulders, and the muscles of his hands clench as they grabbed at him. He felt the loosening of his throat around his cock, and he certainly felt Oliver's deep moan vibrate through them both.

And then Oliver threw himself into his task. He sucked and bobbed and licked at Mal'ik with a messy and artless abandon that made Mal'ik's blood rise and his toes curl. He tightened his fingers in Oliver's hair as he watched the pretty man work him over, pleasure coursing up and down his spine and gathering in his lower belly.

"Good job, Oliver. Fuck, you're beautiful." Mal'ik kept up the praise, and Oliver twisted and let out another desperate sound with every word. Mal'ik could see how hard he was, his cock flushed and glistening, hanging heavily between his thighs. But Oliver didn't make a grab for it; he didn't pay attention to anything but Mal'ik in his mouth.

Soon Mal'ik had to grit his teeth to keep his hips on the bed, every instinct straining to start thrusting into the building, exquisite feeling. "You're going to make me come,

Oliver." A warning as much as a promise, whatever Oliver wanted it to be.

Oliver's fingers spasmed against his skin, and then he popped off Mal'ik's cock. His lips were red and swollen, and saliva glistened all over his mouth. But he didn't pay it any attention. Oliver dragged his nose down to nuzzle at Mal'ik's base. "I just—I want to try something."

Without waiting for a response from Mal'ik or meeting his eyes, Oliver licked down Mal'ik's balls. He took his time, mouthing and kissing at his sac, but he had a clear direction, and Mal'ik's jaw dropped in shock.

When Oliver's tongue brushed his taint, he let out a groan and leaned back and braced his metal hand behind him. With one hand still tangled in Oliver's hair, he tilted his hips to give Oliver better access to his hole.

Mal'ik's heart pounded in his chest. He had never imagined this, and there was something about it that felt wrong and something about it that felt amazing. There was something right about pretty, perfect Oliver covered in a sheen of sweat with swollen lips and a swollen cock burying his face in Mal'ik's ass.

Mal'ik inhaled sharply when Oliver licked a broad stripe right over his hole, and his rim twitched.

Oh fuck, this was happening.

He couldn't remember the last time anyone had eaten him out, and that was Oliver down there.

Oliver licked again, this time probing at his entrance with the tip of his tongue.

Mal'ik twisted his fingers in Oliver's hair, and his thighs shook. "Oh fuck."

He felt rather than heard Oliver's small growl, and that was the only warning he got before Oliver assaulted his hole with his tongue.

Mal'ik snarled and dropped his head back, letting all

his senses narrow down to the wet heat of Oliver licking and sucking at him. And then the invading feel of Oliver thrusting his tongue into him, fighting against the muscle of his rim to get into him.

"Oh god, Oliver. Fuck, that's amazing." Mal'ik's continuous praise was starting to tip over into babbling, and he clenched his metal hand in the bedsheets.

Oliver grunted and dug his nails into Mal'ik's skin. He pressed Mal'ik's thighs wider and pulled his entrance open with his thumbs. He licked deeper into Mal'ik, twisting his tongue around Mal'ik's rim, kissing at him and moaning.

"Oliver." Mal'ik's gasp came out breathy and broken. "Oliver."

Oliver finally left Mal'ik's hole and sucked sloppily back up Mal'ik's cock. He gave his cockhead one last wet suck and then looked up at Mal'ik with wide, desperate eyes.

"Come on me, Mal'ik. Please." Oliver dropped his hand to his own neglected length, and his hips twitched when he wrapped his fingers around it. "Please, like the first time. I want—"

"Fuck yes, Oliver. Anything for you." Mal'ik surged forward and grabbed Oliver's jaw with his metal hand. "Don't stop touching yourself."

He pushed himself from the bed and stood over Oliver to get a good angle, bending Oliver backward until he arched his spine. Oliver whined and started pulling on his own length. Mal'ik held his face tightly, just where he wanted it, Oliver's soft, spit-shined lips just inches from Mal'ik's cock.

Mal'ik started stroking himself, fast and hard, watching Oliver's face twist with anticipation and eagerness.

"Yes, Mal'ik. I want it, please."

Mal'ik growled, and his balls drew up tight and painful. His hand got sloppy. His knees shook.

"Oh fuck, Oliver."

With a yell, Mal'ik burst all over Oliver's beautiful face. White ribbons of his spend landed on Oliver's lips, his high cheekbones, his pointed nose, his forehead. Droplets hung suspended in his eyelashes. Mal'ik milked himself until the weakening spurts missed Oliver's face and landed on his collarbones and chest.

Oliver whimpered and twisted, and his hand jacked desperately over himself. Mal'ik fell to his knees, not even feeling the pain of the impact, and pushed Oliver onto his back.

"I've got you, Oliver. I've got you."

Oliver sobbed when Mal'ik pushed his hand away to take Oliver's length into his own soft hand.

"I've got you. Come for me."

Mal'ik had barely tightened his grip when Oliver's cock kicked against his palm and Oliver was coming with another sob, painting his own chest with milky white. Mal'ik stroked him—his grip slick with cum—until Oliver's cock softened and Oliver started mewling and writhing with the overstimulation.

Mal'ik let out a deep, shuddering sigh and fell forward over Oliver. He braced himself with his metal hand and petted Oliver's hipbone with his soft one. He nuzzled into Oliver's temple, heard Oliver sigh with contentment, and inhaled that sunshine and linen scent.

"You're so beautiful, Oliver. I—" He caught himself, not sure where he'd been about to go. Then he kissed Oliver's forehead. "I love doing this to you."

Before Oliver could reply and before he could come back from whatever blissful, faraway place being painted in cum took him, Mal'ik slipped one arm around Oliver's shoulders, one arm under his knees, and lifted him.

Oliver yelped and quickly wrapped his arms around Mal'ik's neck. "What—what are you doing?"

"Getting you clean." Mal'ik dropped another kiss onto Oliver's forehead and strode the handful of steps into the bathroom.

He set Oliver's feet down on the cool tile, still keeping one arm around his shoulders, and used his free hand to open the stall door and turn the water on. The water in the pipes was still warm from Oliver's last shower, so Mal'ik gently nudged him.

Oliver went quickly and tilted his face up into the spray, then he looked back over his shoulder. When he spoke, his voice was serious rather than sultry. "Thank you, Mal'ik."

Mal'ik smiled, his heart clenching almost painfully in his chest. "Of course."

He turned to leave Oliver to whatever he needed to do to come down—it clearly hadn't involved Mal'ik last time —but then Oliver's wet hand caught his wrist. Mal'ik looked back to see Oliver with a mischievous smile.

"Join me?"

Mal'ik barked out a laugh. "Alright, but don't expect me to be able to do much. I'm not as young as you."

"Standing here naked in the shower with me and looking like a statue of masculinity incarnate is all I ask." Oliver's smirk grew, and Mal'ik flushed hot enough that he knew it was showing even on his dusky skin.

He could smell Oliver's attraction to him—and Oliver had definitely demonstrated an interest in a carnal relationship—but it was different to hear him voice it when neither of them was hard.

He took a step forward, but Oliver stopped him with a hand on his chest before he could get under the water.

"Your arm." He frowned. "Should it get wet?"

Mal'ik glanced at his prosthetic and drummed his metal fingers against his metal thumb. It was the arm of a soldier, made of sturdy stuff and capable of dealing with a little water. But no, it shouldn't really be exposed to a shower if it could help it.

"Not really," Mal'ik admitted. He thought of taking his whole arm off in front of Oliver, breaking the illusion that he was still whole, and he grimaced and shook his head. "But it's fine."

Oliver didn't drop his hand from Mal'ik's chest, even when Mal'ik tried to push past it. "Mal'ik. You've seen my scars. You can show me yours."

Mal'ik looked into Oliver's hazel eyes. He had seen Oliver's scars. Nothing was marring his creamy skin, and Oliver hid them well, but he'd let Mal'ik see them.

Mal'ik's lips twitched in a humorless smile, and he felt the thick line of his own scar tissue pull across his face. "I've never been able to hide them."

"So why are you trying to now?"

It was a fair question. Maybe because when Oliver looked at him the way he did, Mal'ik forgot what he looked like and what he was. And because Oliver made him forget, he had fooled himself into thinking that Oliver didn't notice either. But he did. Oliver saw everything about him, and for now, at least, he was still standing there smiling softly at him.

So Mal'ik inhaled deeply and undid the straps of his harness. Then he grabbed his arm with his soft hand, found the buttons and the latches where it unlocked, and pulled it off. He winced as the nerve endings disengaged with a sharp pain but stifled the grunt.

The arm went limp and dead in his hand, leaving him just a touch off-balance, and he set it on the counter.

He looked back at Oliver to see Oliver staring at his stump, gnarled and studded with ports. But he didn't look disgusted, his head cocked with curiosity. Mal'ik didn't try to step against the hand on his chest this time. Maybe now Oliver had seen it, he wouldn't think Mal'ik could still be his "statue of masculinity incarnate."

But then Oliver's eyes slid up to Mal'ik's, he smiled, and the hand that had been on his chest slid up to the back of Mal'ik's neck. Oliver pulled him forward, under the spray of the water, and then pushed him back against the tile wall.

He slid his wet body up against Mal'ik's and kissed him as insistently as he did everything. Mal'ik moaned, and the fear and stress collapsed out of him. He wrapped his one arm around Oliver's lower back to hold him close as Oliver kissed him eagerly.

Oliver broke the kiss but stayed close. "This is definitely the best way to end sex," he murmured breathlessly against his lips.

Mal'ik chuckled and tightened his hold to press Oliver meaningfully against him, trapping the young human's hardening length between their hips. "You don't seem like you're ending anything."

Oliver smiled sheepishly, and then his brows pinched with pleasure as he rocked his hips against him. "I—I can be quick."

"Can you get yourself off against me, Oliver?" Mal'ik whispered in his ear.

Oliver gave a jerky nod. "Yeah. Yeah, definitely."

"Do it."

Oliver whined and then caught his lips. He started moving his hips against him in earnest, sliding his wet cock over Mal'ik's skin and muscles as he kissed him. Mal'ik could feel the pleasure of the rhythmic motion and friction, but he'd meant what he'd said before—he wasn't young enough to be able to do much.

But he could enjoy the feel of Oliver in his arm, tight against him and straining after his own orgasm.

And he could move that arm down to cup Oliver's ass and slide a long finger between his crack and press the pad of his finger against Oliver's entrance to help him along.

Oliver gasped and sped up his hips, rocking himself between Mal'ik's body and his finger at Oliver's hole. He writhed and whined until he finally cried out against Mal'ik's mouth and his cock twitched hard between them, his rim spasming under Mal'ik's finger.

Any spend was washed away quickly in the water, and Oliver dropped his head against Mal'ik's shoulder with a little laugh.

"Okay, now the sex is over." He lifted his head up with a grin.

Mal'ik shook his head with a laugh. "Youth."

He let Oliver step out of his arm, and they both turned their attention to cleaning off the spit, sweat, and semen from their activities. Most of their attention, at least. Washing interspersed with more kisses, pets, and teasing touches.

When they eventually turned off the shower, Mal'ik grabbed them fresh towels, and Oliver took his with a smile. He toweled his hair and smirked when he caught Mal'ik unable to tear his eyes away from the water droplets dripping over Oliver's collarbone. Then he wrapped the towel around his waist and something loosened in Mal'ik's chest.

The towel Oliver had around his waist was more threadbare, and his skin was paler with a few angry red scrapes standing out in stark relief, but otherwise, he looked just as he had that morning. Clean and smelling of sunshine, with an undercurrent of anxiety.

Without waiting for Mal'ik, Oliver opened the door and stepped out into the bedroom. Mal'ik grabbed his arm off the counter, reattached it, biting down on the hiss of pain, and then followed Oliver into the room to see him looking around with his sharp hazel eyes. "So these are your rooms, then? You live here?"

"Yes." Mal'ik watched as Oliver wandered along the perimeter, investigating the dull, mostly bare walls and the shelves with old training manuals and pictures of old comrades. There were many old things in these rooms, including himself, and Mal'ik felt the weight of his age in the ache of his stump and the youth of Oliver. He pushed the feeling away and let the warmth of Oliver's obvious affection fill the space instead.

Oliver stopped in front of one particular picture and cocked his head at it. "Is that you and Patrick?"

"Yes." From back when Mal'ik still had both his arms.

Oliver leaned forward and squinted at it. "And is that woman Emissary Serihk's bodyguard?"

"Yes. We've been friends for many years."

"Did she get out?" Oliver turned toward him quickly. "I didn't see her or Serihk or Harrison after the explosion."

"I don't know," Mal'ik admitted.

Oliver frowned. "Are you worried?"

"Yes." But Mal'ik had been worried about friends for most of his life. He didn't feel it the same way anymore. If Lar'a was lost, he would grieve, but not before. Oliver frowned at him harder for a second, and Mal'ik caught a whiff of confusion. Oliver turned to continue his patrol but then swung back around.

"Harrison's daughter," he said. "She wasn't on the ship,

but there were other explosions. Do you know if she's okay?"

Mal'ik shook his head slowly. "I don't know."

Oliver scrubbed his hand over his face and sat down heavily on the bed. He lifted his face, hand dragging down it to cover his mouth, and he shook his head. "Fuck." He looked up at Mal'ik. "What the fuck just happened, Mal'ik? What *do* we know?"

The last bit of lingering pleasure drained out of Mal'ik's body. It was time to face reality and leave the hidden nest of pleasure they had built around themselves. He set his towel aside and went to his drawers to pull out clean clothes.

"We know it was a torvar." He pulled on his pants and shirt and turned around as he started doing them up. "We are almost certain it was the Resistance. We know we caught the torvar wearing Governor Tesh."

Oliver let out an almost delirious snort. "Does it reflect poorly on me that I can't think of anyone I'd rather see infected with a brain-eating parasite than Governor Tesh?"

Mal'ik smiled crookedly and felt his scars pull as he walked to his bedside table and picked up his data tablet. "Or poorly on Governor Tesh." He started glancing through the messages from Patrick. "None of the explosions were near the training grounds. If Astrid went there, she should be okay."

Oliver let out a breath and dropped his head back. "That's a relief."

Mal'ik flicked slowly through the information from Patrick. It was the only relief. "There were five bombs. Two to take out the communication towers, two to take out as many government leaders as possible, and one to take out Serihk—or you."

Oliver pressed his palms over his eyes. "Shit. Death toll?"

"Still counting."

"You said two to take out as many leaders as possible?"

"One seems to have been placed under the table of a large meeting."

Oliver stood and paced, running his hand through his hair. "So we can assume that at least that one was very successful."

Mal'ik tracked Oliver as he walked back and forth across the room. "That's probably a safe assumption."

Oliver smelled of stress and despair, but overpowering all of it was an increasingly aggressive scent of frustration.

Oliver flexed and fisted his hands as he walked. When he stopped, his fists were so tight, his knuckles were white, and he glared at the wall. "I get one last chance and it's blown to hell just like the first one. My father won't bother to even look at me again."

Emotion threatened to explode out of Mal'ik's chest, and he reined it in quickly. He stood still: measuring, thinking, marshaling. Oliver's father was a pissant bastard whose opinion meant less than nothing. Mal'ik had no doubt about that.

But he also had no doubt that convincing Oliver not to care was impossible. Mal'ik would have done anything for his father as a child. And then he'd have done anything for the Gat'Raph. He *had* done anything for the Gat'Raph. He had invaded half a planet and slaughtered the humans that stood in his way when he was Oliver's age.

What Mal'ik did have doubts about was where he stood now.

As much as it pained him to admit it, even in the privacy of his own mind, Mal'ik had greater concerns than Oliver and his relationship with his father. As much as he wished he could step in, hold Oliver in his arms and tell him that he would get him through anything, he couldn't. Even if Oliver wanted him to.

Oliver was concerned about a business deal falling through and being on the receiving end of his terrible father's contempt.

Mal'ik was concerned about how many innocent Southern Tava civilians would get caught in the crossfire when the Klah'Eel retaliated against the Resistance.

For a few beautiful days, he and Oliver had occupied the same world, but that was over now.

"Mal'ik?"

Mal'ik pulled himself from his thoughts to see Oliver looking at him, hazel eyes wide and pained.

The data tablet in Mal'ik's hand vibrated, and he looked down at it to see a message from Patrick. "Your bodyguard is on his way to pick you up."

Oliver jerked back. "My bodyg—oh. Garin?"

"Yes."

Whatever Oliver saw in Mal'ik's face made him turn away. "Right. Yes. He's probably falling over himself to sweep me out of here."

"As he should." Because Oliver didn't belong here, not really. He was here for a business meeting, and he was put in danger, and now he would fly far away to somewhere safe and clean and never think of it all again except in cloying, unpleasant memories. And Mal'ik would stay.

He had always known there was no space for him in Oliver's life, but now he realized there was no space for Oliver in his. And that realization made it hard to breathe, but that didn't make it any less true. Mal'ik had people who needed him, and they needed him more than Oliver did.

That didn't mean he didn't yearn for a life with Oliver

by his side. And it didn't mean he didn't care for him with an overwhelming amount of his heart, maybe all of it. He didn't resent Oliver for being far apart from the messy, terrible world that Mal'ik was in. He hoped Oliver would find happiness. The perfect man deserved it.

Mal'ik set the tablet aside and cupped Oliver's face. He stroked his thumb over Oliver's cheek.

"Mal'ik?" Oliver looked up at him with guarded eyes.

Mal'ik inhaled and tried to memorize that special sunshine and linen smell and the feel of Oliver's soft skin under his palm. Then he dropped his hand down to his side. "Garin will be here soon. You should put your clothes back on."

Chapter Seven

OLIVER SAT in the transport ship across from Garin, feeling sick to his stomach.

There were so many things wrong that his mind couldn't find anything to settle on that didn't make him want to curl up in the center of the floor and vomit.

"Oliver." Garin set a hand on Oliver's shoulder, and Oliver jerked back at the feel of it on his shirt.

There was one of the things that was wrong: his dirty, sweaty, bloody clothes scratching against his skin. His skin that had been so nice and clean.

Garin pulled his hand back and lifted it in apology. "Just checking you're alright. We can put off meeting your father if we have to."

There was another thing that was wrong. They were on their way to his father's ship, which had sped to Tava faster than the standard two days it should have taken. That meant his father would have had to put up with more Gs than he liked, which meant he would be in a terrible mood.

He was already going to be in a terrible mood, and

Oliver was going to have to face his wrath barely hours after having the situation blow up in his face—or rather, under his feet.

"No, we can't, and you know it." Oliver hunched in on himself, holding his arm tight over his belly. "You don't make Alistair Turner wait. Not ever."

"There are more important things than Alistair Turner's moods," Garin said lowly, too quiet for the pilot to pick up.

And there was the thing that—somehow—was the most wrong of all.

Mal'ik had thought so too.

He hadn't said it in so many words. In fact, he hadn't said any words at all. But Oliver had seen it in the hardness of his eyes when he'd met them just before Garin barged in. He'd heard it in the coldness of his voice when he'd told Oliver to put his clothes back on.

Except Mal'ik hadn't actually been cold or hard. Oliver dropped his head into his hand and massaged his temples. He just hadn't been soft, comforting, *doting* like he had been before. Because he'd finally seen Oliver—really seen him—and realized how fucking worthless and heartless he was.

He had realized Oliver was the kind of person that focused on his own pain and family strife when other people were dead and dying.

And Mal'ik was better than that. But Oliver wasn't.

"No, there's not, Garin." Oliver lifted his head and met Garin's eyes firmly. "Not to me."

Garin stared at him for a second, then sighed and sat back in his chair. "Alright then."

They spent the rest of the trip in silence as Oliver desperately tried to plug the cracks in his mental wall. He needed to be at the top of his game for this meeting. He could collapse afterward, he could be as pathetic as he needed to be afterward, but right now, he needed to be his best.

By the time the transport docked, Oliver could stand with his shoulders back and his chin up. He stepped out of the ship as though his clothes were still new.

"He's in his office," Garin muttered to Oliver as he passed and led Oliver down the hallway, as though Oliver needed the guidance or the protection.

He had grown up on this ship. The Turner family had estates on all major planets, but they'd spent most of their time on this ship, traveling between his father's various ventures, learning from tutors.

Competing.

Competing for everything. Love, attention, acknowledgment, accolades.

Oliver had always won, but Dominic had always been right behind and he had hated Oliver for it. And Oliver had hated him right back.

Until Oliver had been blown up and Dominic had slid neatly into his place at their father's side.

Oliver could only imagine Dominic's glee at Oliver's second explosion.

Garin stopped at the door to Alistair Turner's office and turned to face Oliver again.

He looked like he was about to say something, so Oliver cut him off with a sneer. "Stop hovering."

He tossed his head down the hallway in a dismissal, then knocked on the door.

"Come in." The familiar words in the familiar deep voice curdled Oliver's stomach, but he'd locked away any of the feelings there, so when he pushed open the door, his hands were steady.

Alistair Turner turned away from a wall of data screens to face Oliver, and the huge—bigger than Oliver had ever seen—grin on his face stopped Oliver dead in his tracks.

His father opened his arms wide. "Oliver! The man of the hour."

Oliver had the strange sense of the world sliding sideways as he stood in the light of his father's bright smile. He opened his mouth to find something to say so he could pretend he understood what was happening. He wanted to seize the opportunity clearly being given to him, but he couldn't even figure out how.

His father beckoned him over. "Come in, come over here. We've got things to plan."

"The next venture?" Oliver's feet brought him to his father's side, and he looked up at the screens to see an array of spreadsheets, figures, and graphs.

His father chuckled. "That's one way to put it."

He clapped his hand on Oliver's shoulder. Oliver couldn't hold in his confusion any longer. His father hadn't done that since Oliver had managed his first intergalactic corporate hostile takeover years and years ago.

"I don't understand. Surely we've lost the contracts. There's no way Southern Tava can support the infrastructure we need to extract the minerals we're looking for."

His father raised his eyebrow at him. "I suppose you haven't seen the news yet. You're right, we've lost that particular opportunity for the moment, but we've got one much better."

His father pulled something up on his data tablet and flicked it up to the largest screen in the center of the wall.

It was a video recording with the odd angle and quality of a satellite capture. Oliver's eyes darted around the screen, trying to find something to orient himself with—

there were buildings, smoke—and then a news channel banner slid across the bottom of the screen.

Ralscoln, Capital City of Southern Tava: 10:40 AM

The new information coalesced the image into something Oliver could understand. Ralscoln, buildings freshly destroyed, fire, and smoke. That was the capital building there in the center of the screen. People were moving around on the roof.

The image cut to another angle, one from the roof itself—a security camera that must have been streaming to an outside server at the time.

A contingent of heavily armed men and women, mostly human, strode across the roof toward the flagpole in the center. A handful of klah'eel guards rushed at them from the other side of the screen, they exchanged fire, and in moments, the far outnumbered klah'eel lay dead.

One man stepped forward and looked down at the bodies. He wasn't tall, but he was broad-shouldered, and his presence dominated the screen. When he lifted his face, Oliver could see that it was rugged and stubbled and handsome in a dangerous sort of way that made Oliver's hackles rise.

He waved the men behind him forward, and they rushed toward the flagpole. Then he looked directly at the camera. He looked long with his eyes narrowed. He wanted his face to be seen. Then he lifted his gun, let the camera stare down its barrel for a second, and the image cut out.

The newsreel returned to the satellite video just as a new flag was hoisted over the capital building. A blank, black, flickering banner that seemed to suck in all the light that hit it.

His father flicked off the video as footsteps approached them from behind.

"Congratulations, Oliver."

Oliver turned to see Dominic walking across the room, a hard smile on his strong features. Dark-haired and blue-eyed, he had the coloring of their mother, striking and attractive but very different from their father. Oliver shared their father's coloring, and it was yet one more advantage he had that Dominic resented him for.

"You've got us a war."

"And there's nothing better for business than a war." Their father pulled the graphs back up on the screen. "Especially now that we're in a better position than the *Wate* Group."

Oliver looked back at the screens, not seeing them. It *was* a war. The Resistance had just raised a flag over the capital of Southern Tava. It might not be a war between two species states, but the Klah'Eel would need to act. They needed to get their land back, and they needed to put down this insurrection they'd allowed to get far too powerful.

Oliver nodded as his mind raced through the opportunity and how all the pieces could fit together. "I've already made the diplomatic connections we'll need. Many of the individuals were probably killed in the attack, but we've still got better access and a stronger network to draw on than any other Human company. Particularly when it comes to Southern Tava."

"Exactly." His father grabbed his shoulder again and beamed up at the screens. Even the feel of the grit and debris pushing into his skin wasn't enough to make Oliver flinch away from that approving gesture.

Dominic came abreast of them and crossed his arms over his broad chest. "And no species state is going to condemn us for helping to put down a terrorist group that threatened our own golden boy."

"No, indeed." Their father shook his head. "PR has already started drumming up support and sympathy for the family. Play our cards right, and we'll be able to ride the wave of goodwill for months." He glanced at Oliver and then pointed at his face. "That scrape is perfect. Make sure a photographer gets a picture of that before it starts to scab."

Oliver frowned and lifted his fingers to his cheek. His skin stung when he made contact just over his right cheekbone. He supposed that probably did strike the right balance between dashing and victimized.

"Like I said, congratulations, Oliver." Dominic smiled at him, because it never did to fight in front of their father, but his blue eyes were like ice.

"Will you be heading back to Earth then, Dom?" Oliver rolled his shoulders back and put his hands on his hips. "Someone will need to hold down the company while Father and I deal with the situation here."

"No. Carson is going to handle that." Their father shook his head. "Dominic has a part to play here."

"An important one, actually." Dominic pulled out his data tablet and started flicking mathematical and chemical formulas onto the screens. "This opportunity comes at the perfect time for my latest project. I—"

"You'll have time for that tomorrow." Their father flicked all of Dominic's work back off the screens and pulled up the headings of Oliver's dossiers. "I want to discuss our diplomatic plan of attack with Oliver."

Oliver saw Dominic swallow before he nodded briskly. "Of course."

Their father waved his hand in the air. "Why don't you go work on your presentation? It will need to be perfect for tomorrow."

If Oliver knew Dominic, he had already been working

on whatever presentation he was giving. For hours longer than he needed to be, obsessing over minutiae and wasting time on likely irrelevant details.

But his brother nodded anyway. "You're right. There are a couple of changes I want to make." Dominic turned on his heel and left the room without waiting for a response, which was good because their father wouldn't give him one.

Alistair Turner had turned his attention back to his next steps and his favorite son.

A twist of pride tangled around Oliver's chest as he watched Dominic stalk away. It had taken him years of disgrace and months of effort and planning to get back to this coveted position. The culmination of all his efforts and all his focus, and he was back at his father's side, basking in his approval, charting out the future of a galaxy.

Oliver swallowed as he turned back to explain the current dossier on the screen to his father.

Everything he wanted and all he could think about was that flag slowly rising over the smoking capital building and the way Mal'ik had looked at him just before he left.

MAL'IK STEPPED out of the general's office, stopped in the hall, and stared at the wall across from him.

He had been a teenager when he'd received his first orders, and they had felt like a gift. Someone had given him an opportunity: a job and a belief in his ability to do it. And for all the years afterward, he had received orders and clarity, purpose, and fulfillment with them.

Sometimes they were difficult. Sometimes they seemed impossible, maybe confusing, maybe frustrating, maybe vague and open-ended. But he had a direction, and he had taken it.

He had never received orders and felt the way he did now.

He turned and walked slowly down the hall, debating his next move. When he got to the next intersection, he took a right instead of the left that would have taken him back to his rooms.

His rooms that still smelled like sunshine and molasses. Mal'ik pushed the thought away before his mind could follow the thread any farther. That was over.

He knocked on a door a few halls later, and Lar'a opened it.

She opened her mouth when she saw him, then closed it, and inhaled deeply through her nose. She frowned then stepped aside. "Get in here."

Mal'ik stepped into the foyer of a small apartment, almost identical to the rooms Oliver had been put up in. The only person he could see was Lar'a, but the door to the study was closed, and the bedroom door was only slightly ajar.

Lar'a grabbed his arm and dragged him to the couch. The couch was set in the same location as the couch in Oliver's quarters: the one he and Oliver had sat on while they ate dinner together. Mal'ik sat on the same side and glanced at where Oliver had been when he'd asked for Mal'ik's advice and told him that his opinions mattered and that his thoughts were valuable, then asked Mal'ik to fuck him, desperate and earnest.

Lar'a sat on the coffee table in front of him, elbows on her knees. "Why do you smell like that?"

"What do I smell like?"

"Don't be coy, Mal'ik," Lar'a growled. "What's going on?"

"It's nothing to do with Serihk or Bryant."

"I didn't think it was." Lar'a narrowed her eyes at him. "They're not the only two people in the galaxy I care about, you know. Tell me what's wrong with you."

Gratitude rushed through Mal'ik's chest at hearing words he hadn't known he needed. He nodded and leaned forward to put his elbows on his knees to match Lar'a's position. "You saw the satellite video?"

"Yeah." Lar'a's upper lip curled, and she bared a fang. "Got a good look at that new Resistance leader we've all been talking about. Fucking scum."

Mal'ik understood her expression. The image of that man and his piercing eyes were seared into Mal'ik's brain, along with an intense hatred of a magnitude he hadn't harbored in a long time. "The general is sending me back."

"To Southern Tava?"

Mal'ik nodded. "He wants me to lead our forces there. To crush the insurrection."

"Good." Lar'a gave that threatening grin Mal'ik had gotten so used to back during the occupation. He hadn't seen it in a while, and it nearly gave him chills now. "Bring the full force of the Klah'Eel army down on their traitorous heads."

"No." The word was out before Mal'ik even thought about it, snapping out of him hard and firm. He stood and paced to the other side of the room, then turned and paced back again. "Not like this. The men they're sending me with, the weapons, the orders I've been given. It's a death sentence for the entire city and every town along the way."

"And so what?" Lar'a shot to her feet as well. "You think those bastards took all of Ralscoln by force? The people there are harboring these traitors. They're helping them. They're just as bad!"

"I cannot go back there as—"

"Enough, Serihk!" Lar'a and Mal'ik fell silent as Bryant's voice snapped out from the bedroom. It was quickly followed by Bryant himself, who slammed open the door and then hobbled out on crutches, a huge cast encasing his left leg from ankle to hip.

He stopped when he saw Mal'ik and Lar'a, chest to chest in the foyer, then just hobbled over to the couch they'd abandoned. "Don't stop on my account."

"Bryant, you—" Serihk strode out of the bedroom, red and black and gray swirling across his cheeks, then stopped as well when he got to the foyer. He stood straighter, and some of the colors receded down his face and back down his neck. "Captain Mal'ik. Can we help you?"

"Sure, help him find some damn sense." Lar'a waved a hand and went to lean against the arm of the couch near Bryant, crossing her arms over her chest.

Mal'ik scowled at her but didn't deny it. Some sense was exactly what'd he come here for. Some sense of what to do, some direction from anyone.

"Well, you haven't come to the right place," Bryant groused from his spot on the couch, his cast-clad leg up on the coffee table. "Sense is in short supply around here."

Both he and Serihk were pouring pungent frustration into the air, but it was tinged with longing and hurt and fear. Serihk closed his eyes and massaged the bridge of his nose with his long fingers. Then he looked up at Mal'ik, and he looked like the confident and competent emissary Mal'ik was used to.

"What's happened, Captain Mal'ik?"

"The Klah'Eel are going back to war with Southern

Tava." Once Mal'ik said the words out loud, something settled in his chest.

"You mean the Klah'Eel are putting down a terrorist group," Lar'a said.

Serihk shot her a look. "It's war by any other name."

"It's worse than a war," Bryant said. "At least wars have rules."

Mal'ik ignored them and kept speaking to Serihk. "I'm being put in charge of the ground force."

"It makes sense." Serihk nodded. "You have much experience with the region, saboteurs, city fighting, and leadership. You're the obvious choice."

Mal'ik dropped his gaze to the floor with a frown. "Yes." He was the obvious choice, and what did that say about him? That he was the obvious choice when someone needed to raze a Southern Tava village. "I can't do it." That certainty that had started to settle settled deeper. "I can't put the people through that."

Lar'a scoffed from her position against the couch. "So you'd rather let them live under the constant shadow of the Resistance's violence?"

"Are the people traitors and *soldiers* of the Resistance, or are they *victims* of the Resistance, Lar'a?" Bryant snapped. "You can't have it both ways."

Serihk shook his head and waved them at them to be quiet. "Regardless, a heavy-handed offensive by the Klah'Eel isn't going to solve any of their problems. Violence will beget more violence. We need a peaceful, diplomatic solution to this problem."

"Are you going to get us that?" Mal'ik asked.

Serihk made a pained face. "I can hardly do it myself. Klah'Eel officials are hawks even during peaceful times. It will take more than me to get them to hold off. I need to get back to the Qeshian senate, find some allies, pull together an interspecies comm—"

"And in the meantime, Mal'ik is ransacking villages and killing civilians." Bryant leaned back and crossed his arms. Red started seething up Serihk's neck, and Bryant held up a hand before he could say anything. "I'm not saying I don't believe in your plan, Serihk. A diplomatic solution is exactly what we need in the long term. I'm just saying it doesn't solve Mal'ik's problem right now."

Lar'a straightened suddenly. "You could be Bryant's bodyguard. We haven't hired anyone yet."

"And after what just happened, no one could blame me for demanding the best." Serihk nodded. "I could talk to some people, pull some strings. There's bound to be push-back against me demanding the proposed head of ground forces for my personal security detail, but I could get it done."

Bryant looked at Mal'ik. "I bet I'd be a way easier charge than Turner. And you'd only have to kill people that needed killing."

The offer was tempting.

The thought of turning his back on his thorny problem and melting into the fold of Lar'a, Serihk, and Bryant made his limbs go loose with relief. He'd have a clear purpose and a meaningful one. Serihk and Bryant did good work; protecting them would be a noble cause.

Shaking his head slowly felt like jumping out of an air transport without checking if his parachute was working.

"I can't do that either. I can't hide away under your wing while this happens." He shook his head more firmly and turned toward the door, catching a glimpse of Lar'a's confused frown as he did so. "Try to stop it soon. I shouldn't have come."

"Captain Mal'ik, what—"

"Shit, Lar'a, stop him!" Bryant's voice cracked through the air, and Mal'ik had just long enough to tense his muscles before Lar'a's hands clamped down on his upper arm and spun him around.

Mal'ik raised his hands. "I'm not doing anything. Let me go, Lar'a."

"Bullshit." Bryant clawed his way up to standing and staggered over to him. "Bullshit, you're not doing anything, and you can't do it alone."

Mal'ik scowled at Bryant, but he couldn't keep it up. Bryant's expression was too earnest, and Mal'ik was too vulnerable. "I can't drag you all into it."

Bryant scoffed. "Tough."

"What are you talking about? What are you doing?" Lara gave Mal'ik a shake, and when he didn't respond, she looked at Bryant. "What is he doing?"

"He's switching sides."

The room fell silent.

All Mal'ik could hear was the pounding of his own heart. His breaths were too shallow to pick up any of the scents in the room.

Lar'a reacted first. She shoved Mal'ik against the wall with a yell. "What?"

She advanced on him, but Serihk stepped between them smoothly. "Calm down, Lar'a." He turned back to Mal'ik. "Are you sure about this?"

Mal'ik had never been less sure about anything. To turn his back on everything he thought he had lived his life for? To betray his leaders and his men and his state?

He nodded. "Those people need me, Serihk." He swallowed and pulled his shoulders back. "I spent too long protecting them to turn my gatlung on them now."

"Fuck…" Lar'a turned away and ran a hand through her hair.

Mal'ik glanced at her but kept looking at Serihk. "I hate the Resistance. I *hate* them. But if I have to join them to protect the people from us, I will."

To Mal'ik's surprise, Serihk just nodded slowly. He didn't look horrified. He didn't even look confused. "It makes sense. You'll be valuable to the Resistance, for the same reasons you would have been valuable to the Klah'Eel."

Bryant leaned heavily on one of his crutches, still standing in the middle of the room. "I think our diplomatic mission just became a lot more urgent, Serihk."

"Yeah, if you can stop the fighting before Mal'ik gets himself killed, that would be great." Lar'a dropped onto the couch and tilted her head back to look at the ceiling. Mal'ik managed a half smile. Concern for his welfare and a lack of physical assault was as good as a blessing coming from her. "Though you know there might be legal repercussions afterward? For being a traitor and all that?"

Mal'ik shook his head. "I can't be bothered by that right now."

"If you even make it to that point." Bryant frowned. "How do you know the Resistance won't just kill you on sight? Why would they trust you?"

"I still have contacts down there," Mal'ik said. "People who I think will vouch for me."

"That's good." Serihk turned away with a sigh. He laced his fingers behind his back and stared off into a corner of the room. Mal'ik inhaled and smelled doubt, fury, and disgust wafting off him, completely at odds with his cool, still demeanor. "Still, I think you'll need something else to prove your goodwill." He turned back around, his skin completely pale but the air around him churning with emotions. "And I think I know what."

"SO you really don't want to give me a summary before we get down there?" Oliver clarified for the last time as he buckled himself into the transport that would bring them back down to Tava.

"It would be a waste of my energy," Dominic replied for the last time as he settled himself and pulled out his data tablet. "You'll hear about it at the presentation just like everyone else."

"Yes, the presentation to our potential clients." Oliver couldn't help himself. If his brother was insisting on undermining and infuriating him, Oliver certainly wasn't going to pay him the courtesy of letting him get some work done during the ride. "After which they'll have questions, and I'll be ignorant."

Dominic didn't look away from his tablet. "Your ignorance of major Turner corporation R&D projects is not my fault."

Oliver laughed in the way he knew Dominic hated and was rewarded by the familiar tick in his jaw. "Your *major R&D project* wouldn't be seeing the light of day if it weren't for my negotiations."

"You mean if it weren't for your habit of getting blown up."

Oliver had been ready for that and let the reference to his traumatic experiences roll off his back. "Call it whatever you want, you admit your little hobbies would go nowhere if it weren't for me carving out opportunities for you. We both know Dad's not very interested in them."

Dominic slammed his tablet into his lap and glared at Oliver. "My *little hobbies* are going to revolutionize the Turner corporation."

"Oh, Dominic." Oliver shook his head with a chuckle.

"You spend too much time alone in your laboratory. Your delusions are showing."

"Fuck you, Oliver," Dominic muttered with a sneer. He seemed to have finally realized Oliver's game and picked up his data tablet again without saying anything more.

Oliver let it drop and let himself look out the window instead. He could only antagonize his older brother so much before even he started to feel guilty. The truth was Dominic really did have a special genius for science and engineering. He had led their R&D department to completion on a number of great projects. And it *was* unfair that their father seemed incapable of seeing that—too dazzled by Oliver's familiar looks and superior charisma to care what his other son did.

Oliver might actually feel bad for Dominic if he wasn't such an arrogant, heartless dick.

Which he supposed was exactly how other people saw him. Well, that was the Turner family for them.

Oliver's mind wandered off into the place he'd been trying to keep it from before he could yank it back. Heartless and selfish—that's what Mal'ik had finally seen.

Fuck it. Oliver watched the surface of the planet approach and finally let himself think about Mal'ik. He must *hate* what was happening. War with Southern Tava? Mal'ik must *hate* it. Oliver could imagine the way his lips would press together, his back would straighten, and his eyes would flash.

Oliver was unabashedly looking forward to seeing Mal'ik at the meeting, though he had no idea what he would do or say. He couldn't make this situation better for Mal'ik, and he highly doubted his presence alone would do it. Mal'ik wasn't interested in his presence any longer. But Oliver needed to see him anyway.

Their transport docked in the same hangar they'd used

when Oliver first arrived in Tava what felt like years ago now. He unbuckled himself, stood and stretched, and checked his clothes for wrinkles. He'd worn something more subdued this time, in honor of the situation, but no less elegant.

Garin met them at the exit to the gangway and spoke to them both but fixed Oliver with a look. "Let me go first."

Oliver just nodded. He wasn't interested in tempting fate at the moment.

Along with Dom's bodyguard, Garin led the way down into the hangar. The group gathered to meet them was small, only a handful of high-up military dignitaries and way more security than last time.

Oliver's eyes traced through the lines of Klah'Eel soldiers wielding gatlungs and rifles, looking for one tall man in particular. But then his gaze caught on Patrick's, and Patrick narrowed his eyes in a knowing, unfriendly way, and Oliver quickly refocused on the dignitaries, feeling exposed.

Dominic ushered them all into the meeting, and Oliver let himself be buoyed along with the dignitaries and bodyguards, nodding and making conversation but not attempting to outshine his brother. Dominic was almost comically eager to get started, though he disguised it well as a somber urgency.

They gathered into a windowless meeting room—the sort that had smart leather chairs designed to make an impression but a darkness designed to emphasize the security of the meeting. Oliver quickly sized up the room as he stepped in.

He and his father had stayed up late into the night deciding exactly who to invite and who to exclude, though, of course, not every attendee had been up to them.

There were ten people total, including Oliver and Dominic.

Serihk and Harrison were already seated, both stoic and tight-lipped. Oliver had wished to exclude them, but the Klah'Eel war minister had insisted on Serihk's presence, and Serihk had insisted on Harrison's. They both glanced at him and then away again without so much as a nod of greeting. Still not allies then.

The gruff-looking older klah'eel man beside Serihk was a general Oliver knew to be a hawk. He had brought the younger klah'eel woman that sat beside him, whom Oliver now recognized as the braided woman who had met with Mal'ik so many times the day before the attack.

The two Klah'Eel dignitaries that had met them in the hangar and took their seats now were rich and powerful and had their own business concerns in Southern Tava.

The most important person, according to Alistair Turner, was the klah'eel man who held himself with an unmistakable air of authority and stood at the podium: War Minister Hashi.

The most important person, according to Oliver Turner, was Mal'ik, who should have been sitting in the empty seat beside Harrison. Instead, Patrick followed them in and stood behind it. Minister Hashi fixed Patrick with a firm glare. "Where is Commander Mal'ik?"

Oliver didn't let the surprise show on his face as he took his seat at the head of the table. Mal'ik had received a promotion then?

Patrick straightened his back and stood at attention. "Commander Mal'ik is in a briefing with his captains, sir. He's evaluating who to bring during the first advance—many of them are too green to have fought in the original campaign. He sent me in his place."

Hashi frowned hard at Patrick, and to his credit, the

human didn't blink. Finally, Hashi nodded, and Oliver's heart sank. "I'll allow it." He pointed a finger at Patrick. "You make sure he gets all of this information, though. He'll need it when he goes down there."

When he goes down there. Who to bring during the first advance. Ice crystallized around Oliver's throat and heart. Mal'ik was being sent to the front. No, Mal'ik was going to be in charge of the front. Oliver fought the sudden urge to stand, flee the meeting, and find him. Mal'ik couldn't go to Southern Tava. It was dangerous. But more than that, it was wrong. Mal'ik couldn't be the one to assault cities; it would break him.

Oliver's eyes darted to the door, and on their way, they caught on Patrick's again. From this close, Oliver saw the open distaste. He forced himself to relax back into his chair. He didn't know what in particular he had done to earn Patrick's dislike—there were so many options after all —but he clearly shouldn't show him any weakness. He would have to find Mal'ik afterward.

Garin had not joined them in the small meeting room, so Oliver typed out a quick order for him to locate Commander Mal'ik as Dominic took the podium. He tucked the tablet away just as Dominic cleared his throat, modeling the respectful attention that every member of the Turner family deserved.

"Thank you for making the time to attend this meeting on short notice," Dominic began, his voice low and even; excellent for conveying competence and confidence in the face of crisis. Dominic might not have the most charisma of the Turner family, but he was no lout when push came to shove. "My name is Dominic Turner. For the past few years, I have been leading a project at the Turner Corporation Research and Development Department that we hoped would never see the light of day."

Lies. Dominic was chomping at the bit to unleash on the world whatever it was he'd been working on, but even Oliver almost believed his serious, sad blue eyes.

"But unfortunately, I believe its day has come." Dominic made a few swipes on his tablet sitting on the podium's surface, and the screen behind him filled with an aerial image of Ralscoln still burning, rubble in the street, and a black flag flying over its capital building.

He paused for a moment—to let the image settle in—and Oliver took a quick read of the room. Serihk, Harrison, and Patrick looked unmoved, likely ready to reject any Turner proposals out of hand. But the klah'eel in the room looked suitably unnerved, angry, or determined. They were ready.

Oliver only hoped whatever Dominic had cooked up wasn't too horrifying.

"Your enemies are tenacious, driven, organized," Dominic continued. He swiped a few more images onto the screen—a group of rebels at target practice with obliterated dummies that had once had tusks, a refinery with that black flag over it, and then a shot familiar to all of them now: the intense stare of the Resistance leader. "And worse: fearless. I can fix that for you."

Low murmurs rustled around the room, too soft to hear, but Dominic's eyes lit up.

"Fear can bring down a force's defenses faster than orbital bombardment and with infinitely less structural damage. It can cause loyal men to flip, sow discord in the ranks, and erode trust. It impedes tactical decision-making and compromises leaders."

"And fear"—Dominic threw up a slide full of chemical formulas and the diagram of a large organic compound that Oliver didn't bother trying to understand—"is biological."

More murmurs. Oliver was beginning to see where Dominic was going with this, but his brother continued before he could wrestle with the ramifications.

"My team and I have developed an aerosolized compound that when inhaled produces staggering results in human, qesh, and klah'eel test subjects." Dominic paused with his finger poised over his tablet. "I warn you: the following videos are disturbing."

Disturbing did not cover it.

A human man sobbing and screaming in the corner of a sterilized white room with such a profound look of terror, Oliver felt the hairs on the back of his neck rise.

A mottled brown-yellow qesh shrieking and clawing a window open before disappearing out of it.

A klah'eel tearing at his own nose. A human with a gun to her own head. A human unloading a gun into the heads of—

Oliver looked away.

He swallowed and breathed against the sounds he still heard.

How had Dominic even gotten permission to conduct such experiments? How had he managed to override his humanity to carry them out?

Eventually, the screaming of the last video ended with the echoing of a gunshot, and blessed silence fell over the room.

"As you can see," Dominic said quietly, "it is quite potent. These were not civilians. These were hardened criminals, both civilian and military."

So that's how he had gotten the permission. No one cared what you did with death row inmates. Maybe someone should have.

"Modern gas masks aren't effective. The compound is very small." Dominic returned to the slide of chemical formulas and diagrams. So innocuous. It might as well be the slide for the latest anti-aging pill. "A completely sealed hazmat suit would be effective, but Southern Tava doesn't have enough of those to clad an entire organization in, and you can easily blockade the area to prevent the raw materials required to make them from entering the region."

Oliver glanced at Minister Hashi, who nodded thoughtfully. Dominic had already won. Goddamn it. Oliver was the one that had insisted on Minister Hashi being here. He'd known Hashi would go for anything that might give him a leg up no matter how brutal.

"What about application?" Oliver spoke before he could stop himself. "How would you subject a single force or group without affecting surrounding civilians? Or your own men?"

Dominic's eyes flashed with pure hatred for a moment before his cool demeanor covered it over. "The compound is light, but it can bind with different mediums without losing effectiveness. It could be applied using a simple grenade filled with heavy gas for targeted operations. Or dropped in a timed capsule from orbit to disperse over a large area." Dominic turned away from Oliver and toward Hashi instead. "That would be entirely up to you and your men, sir."

Entirely up to Mal'ik. Oliver's throat tightened. Mal'ik was the one who would be deciding to dose people with literal fear. To terrorize them. To drive them mad.

"And do people recover?" Serihk spoke suddenly but mildly, as though he were merely curious. "After they've been subjected to your compound."

"Completely," Dominic nodded. "Aside from any physical injury they may have sustained during the experience, they return to themselves within a few hours of coming out of contact with the compound."

"Completely?" Harrison crossed his arms, and Oliver saw the moment Dominic registered his uneducated accent in the tick in his jaw. "They recover completely from the most terrifying moments of their lives?"

Dominic narrowed his eyes at him. "There may be some lingering effects on the subjects' psyches, but our tests have found no evidence of degraded mental faculties."

"Did you look for any evidence?" Oliver asked.

Dominic's eyes cut back to him.

Their father would make Oliver pay for this when Dominic reported back, but he didn't drop his gaze.

"We did," he replied. "It may sometimes be useful to extract knowledge from those previously affected by the compound, and so we had to confirm that subjects would still be capable of relaying such valuable information."

Minister Hashi clapped both palms onto the surface of the table. "That's all I needed to hear."

It was done.

"Mr. Turner, I think you may have just given us the means to finally reclaim our land from these lawless men who have been thorns in the side of the Klah'Eel empire for decades." Hashi stood and returned to the podium with his hands outstretched.

Dominic took it and shook it firmly. "I sincerely hope so, sir."

"You'll be able to produce enough for our use here on such short notice?"

"Absolutely. We have an excellent production line."

They did. Oliver had overseen the acquisition of an excellent chemical production facility himself, two systems away. If they used high-speed freight, the product could be here in days, ready to be loaded into canisters and unleashed onto unsuspecting civilians.

Not that Mal'ik would ever allow that.

Dominic turned back to the small audience.

"Are there any other questions?"

The female klah'eel with the braids raised her hand and asked something, but Oliver wasn't paying attention anymore. He needed to get to Mal'ik. He needed to get the man out of this situation. Maybe Oliver could hire him as personal security or heavily suggest him to the president of a well-established mercenary corporation that Oliver was friendly with because they were rivals of Wate.

Mal'ik was a loyal Klah'Eel soldier, and Oliver didn't doubt his honor, but surely it was exactly that honor that would torture Mal'ik if he was forced to be the blunt tool the Klah'Eel empire used to crush a simple uprising.

Oliver pulled his tablet out, not caring how it looked anymore, and checked the message from Garin. He paused and read it again.

Mal'ik wasn't at the meeting with his captains.

He had sent a high-ranking captain in his stead so that he could attend a confidential security briefing with the war minister.

This confidential meeting.

At which Patrick was representing him.

Oliver lifted his eyes slowly to look at the human. Patrick must have felt his eyes on him because he glanced Oliver's way after a moment. He had a death glare to rival Dominic's, and it made Oliver's blood run cold and his skin clammy.

Something was wrong. Something was wrong with Mal'ik, and Patrick knew what it was.

He let his eyes trail over Harrison and Serihk. Harrison looked like he was just barely keeping his anger locked behind his strong jaw. Serihk looked as unflustered as ever, not a swirl of color over his skin. Did they know what it was? Perhaps.

Oliver met Patrick's glare with a cool stare of his own. Patrick would be the easier one to break.

Oliver tried to focus on the rest of the meeting. Important information was being exchanged. Information he might need in the future. But all he could think about was the way Mal'ik had looked at him when they parted.

Distant. Apart. Dismissive. Sad?

Oliver should have done something then. He shouldn't have let them part like that. Like they would never see each other again and like Oliver was okay with that. And now something had happened and it—

Oliver shoved the feelings away again and again. He would fix this.

As soon as the meeting ended and Dominic finished up his last words—pretending he wasn't loving every second of this—Oliver stood and left the room. He saw Dominic open his mouth to call him back, but Oliver let the door close behind him before he could do so. Dominic would be stuck chatting with their clients. Oliver had someone else to catch.

Once out into the hall, he spun around and leaned against the stone wall. He crossed his arms and watched the door. The braided klah'eel woman came out, shot him a look, and then continued on her way.

Next was Patrick.

"Smith." Oliver straightened as soon as the man came out. "I need to speak with you."

"Turner." Patrick's upper lip curled, and if Oliver had had any doubts about how Patrick felt about him, he didn't have them anymore. "I've got nothing to say to you."

Oliver stepped in front of him as he tried to walk down the hall. "You've got at least one thing. And I'd bet a lot more."

Serihk's voice sliced over them, calm and persistent as always. "Is something wrong here?"

Oliver felt a fresh burst of hatred for the meddling qesh. "Nothing. Smith and I just need to chat."

"Smith's busy." Harrison appeared at Serihk's side, and Oliver was stunned silent for a moment. It hadn't been visible while they'd been sitting, but Harrison's left leg had a thick cast from ankle to hip. Oliver was reminded forcefully of just how lucky he was to have escaped the explosion as unscathed as he had.

How lucky he was to have been saved.

He sighed and gentled his voice. "Look, it won't take long. It's important." And just for good measure, because he never used this word, "Please."

Patrick looked torn. Harrison as well. Serihk, of course, did not. "Smith really doesn't have the time to spare. He—"

"I do," Patrick interrupted him.

Serihk's eyes widened, but he recovered quickly. "You don't."

"I do." Patrick shot Serihk a glare, and Serihk looked like he was about to respond harshly, red sliding up his throat, when Harrison put a hand on his forearm.

"Patrick knows his own schedule, Serihk." He gave the qesh an awkward tug as he swiveled on his crutches. "Let's go. Take care, Patrick."

"I will." Patrick nodded, then looked at Oliver and jerked his head to a door that hung slightly ajar a couple of rooms down. "In there."

Oliver tried not to physically let out a sigh of relief as he followed Patrick into the room and shut the door behind him. He flicked the lights on. "I know Mal'ik wasn't at the meeting you said he was at."

Patrick planted his feet and crossed his arms. "Yes, he was."

Was that how a soldier lied? Oliver rolled his eyes. "No, he wasn't. And he wouldn't have gotten confused, and he wouldn't have lied to you. So, where is he?"

"That's his business."

"And I'm making it mine."

"You don't own him, Turner." Patrick strode forward and jabbed a finger into Oliver's chest.

Oliver scowled and batted the bigger man's hand away. "Don't try to get macho on me, Patrick. I want to help him."

Patrick barked out a laugh and turned away. He put his hands on his hips and looked at the ceiling, shaking his head. "Yeah, I'm sure you do." His tone said otherwise. "Don't worry, you and your brother have helped enough."

Oliver grimaced, though he knew Patrick couldn't see it. He glanced over his shoulder, as though anyone else was in the room with them, before admitting, "I don't feel good about it. The gas."

Patrick snorted. "Sure you don't."

Oliver grabbed Patrick's arm and yanked him around to face him. "I don't want Mal'ik to use it."

Patrick frowned at him. "Why not?"

"Because he'll hate it."

Patrick didn't reply right away, eyes narrowing as they searched through Oliver's.

Oliver wasn't sure what he was going to see. He wasn't sure what was there.

"And that matters to you?"

"Yes." Oliver swallowed. "Immensely."

Patrick stared at him for a few more moments, then nodded slowly. Oliver's chest started to loosen, but then

Patrick smiled grimly. "Well, don't worry then. He won't use it."

And then he pushed past Oliver and out the door.

"Patrick." Oliver slammed the door open to chase him. "Patrick!"

But Patrick was striding fast down the hall, and Oliver wasn't about to make a scene. He stopped in the doorway, watching the human's broad back as he left, hands clammy and head spinning. *He won't use it.*

"What the hell was that, Oliver?" Oliver's eyes refocused on Dominic standing outside the meeting room with his bodyguard and Garin. Oliver swallowed, glanced one last time down the hall to see Patrick disappearing around a corner, and then scowled at Dominic.

"I should be asking you that." He gestured at the room they had held the meeting in and kept his glare on Dominic as the four of them started back to the transport. "What sort of sick thing was that?"

"What?" Dominic's jaw dropped in genuine surprise.

"What sort of fucked up person makes something like that?" Oliver pressed. "*Tests* something like?"

Dominic stopped in his tracks and stared at him. For a moment, Oliver thought he saw real hurt in his eyes, but it was gone in an instant. "Fuck you, Oliver. Since when do you care about our experiments? How dare you call me— You know what, no." Dominic held up a hand. "I don't care. Just fuck you."

And then he kept walking, hand still up as he walked past Oliver as though to keep himself from seeing Oliver's face.

Oliver inhaled deeply before following. Fuck him, indeed.

He won't use it.

Patrick's words sat like lead in Oliver's stomach. No,

more like titanium or tungsten. Something immutable, immalleable, and undeniable.

The more Oliver tried to convince himself that Patrick didn't mean what Oliver thought he meant, the more he became sure.

Chapter Eight

OLIVER STOOD under the hot spray of the shower until the rhythmic pounding of the water numbed his shoulders. Finally, he reached out and turned it off. Hot water wasn't going to save him from his anxiety this time. It turned out being clean didn't make everything all better, even with his silk washcloths and earth lavender soaps.

He stepped out, dried, and slicked his hair back from his face. He never had taken that picture his father wanted, and now the scrape over his cheek was an unsightly minor wound, red in the center and surrounded by the pale white of dead skin. He tilted his head back and forth and looked at himself in the mirror.

Oliver Turner.

The face in the mirror looked much the same, but the only thing that felt familiar about himself was the unease in his stomach. Everything had started to tilt when he'd seen that disappointed look in Mal'ik's eyes. And then Oliver had finished flipping his world upside down just an hour ago, in his father's office.

He could still change his mind.

Oliver looked at himself a second longer in the mirror and then shook his head and returned to his bedroom.

He couldn't.

He opened his wardrobe and paused. He ran his hands over all the fine fabrics. He really did love his clothes. Then he picked out his outfit: formal enough for a political dinner that in part was to celebrate and seal the fantastically lucrative deal between the Turner family corporation and the Klah'Eel empire, and yet somber enough to show that he did still remember that this was about war.

He paired it with a heavy pendant that was a bit out of style now but the right size. He was glad he hadn't gotten rid of it, though he'd considered it several times. Something about the fine filigree of silver along its outside had always persuaded him to keep it.

He checked his pendant, his pockets, his data tablet, that his boots were tied. Everything was orderly and in place. He looked around his room and swallowed. He felt certain he was forgetting something or that he should bring more. He fingered his pendant and nodded decisively. There was nothing else.

He stepped out into the hallway and closed the door of his bedroom.

Garin stood outside his door. "Back down to Tava?"

"Have my brother and father left their ship yet?" Oliver was back on his personal ship to prepare for the dinner.

Garin tapped his tablet a few times. "No, they're still in their rooms. They're due at their hangar soon, though."

"Let's go there. I'd like to meet them." Oliver turned and started walking toward his own transport ship. "We'll go back down to Tava together."

A short transport ride later and Oliver was stepping out

into the Turner family ship's hangar just as his brother and father were entering from the living quarters.

"So, you've decided to join us after all?" Dominic raised an eyebrow when he saw Oliver. His eyes had been even icier than usual after their tiff leaving the meeting room. He'd clearly been eager to throw Oliver under the bus to their father as soon as they arrived, but Oliver had beaten him.

He'd told his father that Dominic had done brilliantly, that he'd had an answer for every question, that he had knocked the softballs Oliver had lobbed him out of the park. In the face of that glowing praise and the obvious explanation for Oliver's needling in the meeting, Dominic had been able to do nothing but demure.

"Of course." Oliver joined them in the larger transport. "The Turner family should present a united front."

"Good." Their father nodded crisply. "We wouldn't want the Klah'Eel thinking that any disagreement they might have witnessed in the meeting was evidence of discontent within the ranks."

Dominic and Oliver met each other's eyes only briefly before settling back into their chairs. They rode in silence until their father spoke up again suddenly, though he kept his gaze trained out the window.

"I'm proud of both of you."

Stunned silence.

"Everything you boys have accomplished. What *we've* accomplished, as Turners, together. I'm very proud."

Both Oliver and Dominic froze, faces neutral but still. They had never heard those words before. *I'm proud of both of you.*

Their father had said he was proud of them each individually, but it had always served two purposes: to praise one and to remind the other to do better. They didn't have a family script for *I'm proud of both of you.*

Dominic found his voice first. "Thanks, Dad."

Oliver swallowed around the lump in his throat and fought the urge to touch the pendant against his breastbone. "We do our best."

"And then some." Their father still hadn't looked away from the window, and Oliver could just make out his face in the reflection. There was more emotion in it than Oliver had ever seen—not a lot, certainly—he was still Alistair Turner—but more.

The rest of the journey continued in a new kind of silence, tense, uncertain, and fragile. Oliver and Dominic's eyes flickered to each other a few times, but they never spoke. Then they arrived at the grand hangar in the political estate on Tava, and the strange mood was broken.

"Alright." Their father stood, rolled his shoulders a few times, and cracked his neck. Oliver wondered if all the posh and powerful people their father interacted with knew he went into every encounter as though going into an athletic match. "You've both received your dossiers and reviewed them?"

"Yes, sir," Dominic said, and Oliver nodded as they both stood and stretched out the stiffness from the transport journey. Ever since they had been children, they had received dossiers going into dinners and diplomatic events. They were assigned individuals to approach and engage in conversation and topics to steer those conversations.

Oliver had always had more than Dominic, and while it had been a lot of work for a child, it had been the early evidence of their father's favoritism.

Oliver had so loved being the favorite.

"Good. Let's go." Their father led the way down the

gangway—none of the bodyguards dared to insist on being first with their father.

They made their way through the complex, and Oliver felt a strange feeling of nostalgia once they started walking through arcades he recognized. He had criticized that standing puddle of water every time he had passed it and watched Mal'ik's little smile twitch around his tusk. It had been silly then, but it seemed even sillier now when just across the courtyard were still smoldering ruins.

Something hit him in the gut when they passed the courtyard where Oliver had first met Governor Tesh. Had he been the torvar even then? And that was the corner that Mal'ik had dragged him around to tell him to put his scent cream on. It was such a little thing, but Mal'ik had gone out of his way to protect and support Oliver, and that had meant an embarrassing amount to him.

Oliver touched his throat. He had laid his cream on thick again today.

Eventually, they arrived at the banquet. Their father looked them both up and down, nodded, *smiled*, and then they made their entrance.

Oliver's nerves burst to life in his stomach as soon as he stepped across the threshold. He took a deep breath.

It was cocktail hour. This was when they would be able to do the most of their mingling, though there would be time after dessert as well. But Oliver couldn't wait that long —in truth, he couldn't wait even until the end of cocktails.

As much as he wished he could grab a drink and work down his assignment list like he always had, he had a much more important and much more urgent task. One he couldn't draw too much attention to.

Conveniently for him, Bryant Harrison was on his list.

Emissary Serihk didn't look like he was planning on leaving Harrison's side for a moment, though. Oliver took a glass of a bubbling light wine from a passing waiter and drifted into the corner, watching them. Serihk wasn't on any of the Turners' lists—no one wanted to engage with him, least of all Oliver.

But Oliver might have to if the qesh refused to leave off carrying around his human consultant's drink and fussing over the little napkins the waiters with the hors d'oeuvres kept trying to pass him and whether he could hold them and his crutches at the same time.

For what it was worth, Harrison looked quite capable of managing crutches and drinks at the same time, and his dark brows gradually descended lower and lower over his piercing eyes. Finally, he turned to Serihk firmly, said some things that made Serihk press his lips together tightly, snatched his little napkin from Serihk's long fingers, and then hobbled on his own over to a decadent table of refreshments.

Oliver didn't waste any time casually making his way over to the table and plucking a little berry wrapped in some sort of fragrant leaf from the platter Harrison was eyeing. "You don't look like you're enjoying yourself."

Harrison eyed him, then grabbed two berries, holding one in his napkin and stuffing another into his mouth. "And you look like you're enjoying yourself too much."

"Looks can be deceiving." Oliver chuckled. He popped the berry into his mouth, and a surprisingly pleasant sweet and savory flavor burst over his tongue. It was hardly correct to stand next to the table and gorge himself, but Harrison didn't seem like the type to appreciate correctness anyway, so Oliver took another and ate that one too. "Honestly, I find these sorts of events draining."

"Really?" Harrison raised an eyebrow. "I thought working events like this was your whole thing."

Oliver shrugged. "It's not my whole thing, but yes, I'm good at it. Doesn't mean I like it."

A beat passed, and Oliver realized he didn't think he'd ever told anyone that before. He frowned. Such a simple truth about himself, and he'd never actually told anyone.

"How is your daughter?" he asked before he could dwell on it more. "She left the ship before it…"

"Exploded, yes." Harrison ate two of the leaf-wrapped berries at the same time, licked the juice off the pad of one of his calloused fingers, and then waved his hand. "She's fine. Already on her way to Klah. She won't see any fighting—not this time around at least."

Oliver sighed, thinking of the smile in Mal'ik's eyes when Astrid had shown him her gatlung. "That's good."

"Yup." Harrison hobbled a few plates down to what looked like cheese cubes, and Oliver followed him. "So what are you doing hiding out here at the snack bar with me? Trying to avoid this draining event?"

"Not quite." Oliver picked out a cube. Tangy. Not bad. "I need something from you."

Harrison didn't bother to look at him, surveying the cheese plate. "You want to know where Mal'ik is."

Oliver's throat constricted, and he fought the urge to glance over his shoulder to see if there was anyone around that might see whatever emotion had surely just overtaken his face. He waited a moment until he was sure his voice wouldn't crack. "Yes."

Harrison selected a slice of creamy white cheese but only set it on his napkin as he awkwardly turned in place to face Oliver fully. "And you think I'll tell you?"

"I'm hoping you will," Oliver said honestly. But that seemed inaccurate, not forceful enough. He mentally filed through all possible ways he could put weight behind the statement: threatening, coercing, bribing, cajoling. Those were his usual tactics, and he knew they would never work here. He had only one tactic left, and he had never used that one before. Vulnerability. "Actually, I'm begging you to."

Harrison's eyebrows rose to his hairline. "Begging, huh? You ever done that before?"

"No." No, Oliver had never thrown himself at the mercy of anyone. He wasn't even sure Harrison was the merciful type.

Harrison's brows lowered again, and he stared at Oliver for a few moments. Oliver let him stare, feeling almost as exposed as when caught around a klah'eel without any scent cream. Once the urge to fidget was about to become unbearable, Harrison huffed a laugh. "That Mal'ik really did a number on you, didn't he?"

Oliver frowned, trying to discern if anyone had just been insulted. It was the truth, though, wasn't it?

The strong, kind, gentle, upstanding man had stepped into Oliver's life, shown him what it was like to be cared for and to care, and changed everything forever. Oliver could never go back to being the sort of man that would let Mal'ik go out into a dangerous world alone and unprotected while Oliver sat in comfort and luxury and provided the weapons to be used against him.

"Yes, I suppose he did."

Harrison gave him an almost abashed half smile, and his eyes flicked over to Emissary Serihk, who was talking to a Klah'Eel diplomat but clearly angled in such a way as to keep an eye on them. "Lucky for you, I know a thing or two about posh men who get too attached to the rougher sorts for their own good."

Emissary Serihk could apparently take it no longer, and after glancing at them to see them both looking at him, he excused himself and made his way over to the sidebar they stood at. He opened his mouth when he got close, but Harrison beat him to it.

"Tell him where Mal'ik is."

Serihk's mouth snapped closed again. He straightened his back and laced his fingers behind him. He looked at them both, then nodded to one of the side rooms that lined the hall.

They filed into the room, Oliver exchanging his empty glass of wine for a full one along the way, and then shut the door behind them.

"Why would I do that?" Serihk asked, turning back around to face them. Harrison stood next to Oliver, just a little taller even when hunched in his crutches, and it wasn't lost on either Oliver or Serihk whose side he was standing on.

"Because I want to help him," Oliver said. "I know he's joining the Resistance."

Serihk didn't miss a beat. "And what makes you think something as ridiculous as that?"

"Because he's not here. No one's seen him." Oliver sighed. "And because he's a good man."

"Too good for the likes of you, don't you think?"

"Serihk!" Harrison snapped, but Oliver was already nodding.

"Yes." That wasn't so difficult to admit. Oliver had always known that. "But I'm still here. I just want to help him. I need to help him. I can't abandon him now. But I need your help."

Serihk looked at him, something in his eyes softening. He glanced at Harrison—or more accurately at Harrison's horribly broken leg—then back at Oliver. He shook his head. "You think you can protect him. Trust me, it won't work out the way you think it will."

Then he turned away toward the private bar cart at the

back of the room, and Harrison let out a sigh and went to him.

Oliver bit his tongue as he watched Harrison grab Serihk's upper arm and pull him close. His big hand ran up the tall qesh's arm to the back of his neck and tugged his head down so he could speak softly to him—too softly for Oliver to hear. Oliver watched Harrison's thumb smooth circles over Serihk's nape as swirls of gray eddied with purple just under his collar.

Serihk said something, and Harrison shook his head, his thumb still stroking softly. Finally, Serihk nodded and glanced over his shoulder at Oliver. He straightened up as Harrison's hand dropped off and clasped his hands behind his back again.

"You're very convincing, Turner, I'll give you that," Serihk said. "But Mal'ik's survival and success during the next few hours rely on secrecy. What do you have to convince me to trust you other than a sob story?"

Oliver took a deep breath and lifted the chain of his heavy pendant over his head. He held it out to Emissary Serihk. "This."

———

MAL'IK CALMLY WALKED down the hall, gatlung slung over his shoulder more as a security blanket than anything else. If anything went wrong at any point in the next couple of hours, a gatlung was going to do him no good.

"Cap—Commander Mal'ik." The guards on either side of the door to the holding cell stood at attention when they saw him.

Mal'ik nodded at them. "All quiet?"

"Yes, sir."

"Has anyone spoken to him?"

One guard nodded. "Smith and Teav both have, sir."

The other guard made a face. "Though I don't think they got anything out of him by the way they smelled when they left."

Mal'ik knew for a fact they hadn't gotten anything. And they hadn't been surprised. This wasn't the torvar's first stint in a holding cell.

"Alright, I'll take it from here. Smith needs you both at the banquet. They're opening an extra room and we need a couple more feet on the ground."

The first guard nodded crisply and turned to start walking down the hall, but the second hesitated.

"Excuse me, sir, but a torvar should always be guarded by two men at least." He shifted from foot to foot and grimaced. "So that the second one can raise the alarm if the first one gets taken, or at least…kill him."

Mal'ik clasped his shoulder. "I know. I've fought a few torvars before, during the occupation." The memories still sent chills down his spine. "Don't worry. I won't open the door."

The second guard looked like he was going to continue to be a problem, but he eventually nodded and turned to follow his partner. "Good luck, sir."

"And to you."

Mal'ik watched them walk down the hall and turn the corner. Then he waited for a beat before opening the door.

The holding cell was blindingly bright, with so many white lights as to obliterate any shadows, giving it an eerie, otherworldly feel. Mal'ik blinked as his eyes adjusted and could then take in the expected wall of glass that separated him from the dark mass of Governor Tesh. The klah'eel was tied tightly to a chair, his arms behind his back, and a thick metal collar wrapped around the entire expanse of his neck.

At the sound of Mal'ik closing the door behind him, the governor's head lifted, and Mal'ik met the eyes of someone who was very much *not* Governor Tesh. The torvar wearing a klah'eel's body lifted his chin and let his dark hair fall out of his eyes, lips twisting in a smirk around tusks. The torvar were masters at disguise, deception, and camouflage. But this torvar wasn't even trying, not right now at least. He let the sickening incongruence show through.

Mal'ik narrowed his eyes. "Is Tesh even still in there?"

The torvar lifted a single shoulder. "Who could say? He wasn't a very forceful personality to begin with."

Mal'ik didn't have an answer to that. His feet wanted to stay rooted to the spot or to turn and run. His mind wanted some reassurance that he was safe, that his mind and body would remain his own. But his brain knew he didn't have the time for either.

He forced himself to step up to the heavy glass door that separated them and opened the keypad. "I need you to take me to your leader."

The torvar straightened up at that, his languorous posture dropping off like a blanket.

"And why would I do that?"

"Because I have useful skills and experience. I'm Cap—"

"I know who you are," the torvar cut him off. "Mal'ik of Klah. Part of the original force that invaded Southern Tava. Part of the occupying force for years afterward. Surprisingly popular with the locals for all that you were one of the bad guys—some of them are still in contact with you. Getting on in years now, some would say past your prime, but they wouldn't say it very loudly. One of the likely picks for commander once we started this war." The torvar cocked his head. "Did that not happen?"

Mal'ik glanced up from the keypad to the torvar, not giving it the satisfaction of seeing him discomfited. "It did."

"Was the promotion not enough?" the torvar asked as though they had the time to analyze Mal'ik's motivations.

"I'm not interested in a promotion." Mal'ik input the code to unlock the glass door. He paused, steeled himself, and then pressed enter. "I'm not interested in working for the Klah'Eel anymore at all."

The torvar leaned forward as the glass door released with a hiss, though his wrists were still bound behind the back of his chair. "You're interested in joining the Resistance?"

Mal'ik's lip curled. He had never thought the answer to that question would be yes.

The torvar laughed. "Oh and you look so happy about it."

"I'm interested in protecting the people." Mal'ik circled the torvar to get a look at his wrists. They were bound to either end of a spacer so that one couldn't help untie the other. The skin under the zip ties wasn't chafed, meaning the torvar hadn't been struggling. Mal'ik didn't know if that was because the torvar knew he could never get out or if it was because he knew he could and didn't need to struggle. The latter wasn't a comforting thought. "And you're my only option right now."

"Maybe, but you're not *our* only option." The torvar glanced over his shoulder at him. "You'd be useful, don't get me wrong, but why should we trust you?"

"Because I'm here doing this." Mal'ik unslung his gatlung and used the blade at the end to cut each of the torvar's wrists free.

The spacer dropped to the ground with a clatter, and the torvar brought his hands back around to the front and massaged them. "A compelling piece of evidence, I'll give you that."

"What's your name?"

"What?" The torvar stood and turned to face him.

"What's your name?" Mal'ik slung the gatlung back over his shoulder. "We're about to steal a ground transport and betray our country together. I'd like to know your name."

"*Your* country." The torvar dropped his wrists back down. "What, your intelligence units haven't even figured out my name yet?"

"No one uses it. You're just called 'the torvar.'"

"And that's not good enough for you?"

"No."

The torvar put his hands on his hips and shifted his weight so that his left hip cocked out slightly. It was a distinctly un-klah'eel-like mannerism, and it gave Mal'ik another twinge of discomfort to see Tesh's body doing it. "Sebastian."

"Sebastian? That's very—"

"Human, yes." The torvar—Sebastian—nodded. "I was raised in a human body. Shall I tell you about my mother as well? Maybe the little dog I had growing up? Or are we escaping?"

Mal'ik pressed his lips together. "We're escaping."

"And this too?" Sebastian pointed to the metal casing around his neck. It could be unlocked with the same code used to open the door.

Mal'ik hesitated.

Sebastian sighed. "Fine. Later then."

Relieved Sebastian wasn't going to press the issue, Mal'ik led the way back into the empty hall. He wasn't particularly convinced that the metal casing effectively kept a torvar locked inside a body. The neck might be the optimal and preferred way for the worms to enter and exit hosts, but Mal'ik doubted it was the only way, especially for one as experienced in body-hopping as Sebastian. Still, he wasn't ready to give up that line of defense completely.

Sebastian looked back and forth down the hall, then swept an arm out in front of him. "After you, Commander Mal'ik."

"Just Mal'ik," Mal'ik muttered as he passed him. He was giving up his titles. They no longer applied.

Sebastian didn't comment, and they hastened toward the farther—and emptier—transport bay on the south side of the complex. Sebastian managed to move nearly silently even in a klah'eel's body, and Mal'ik found himself frequently looking over his shoulder to make sure he was still there. He always was, right on Mal'ik's heels.

If Sebastian could defeat the neck casing, it would be the easiest thing in the world for him to abandon Tesh's body and burrow into the nape of Mal'ik's neck.

But he didn't.

"Almost there," Mal'ik told him as they rounded the last corner—still unseen. Patrick had arranged the guard's patrols and postings to give him this opening, and Mal'ik felt a surge of gratitude and loss.

"I know. I assume you have some supplies stashed somewhere?"

"Yes." Mal'ik opened the doors to the transport bay. "In—"

He froze.

The slim figure in the middle of the transport bay turned toward them, and Mal'ik felt as though he had taken one of Lar'a's punches to the gut. Or maybe one of Patrick's kicks. The air rushed from his lungs, and the contents of his stomach rolled and threatened to follow.

"Oliver."

"Mal'ik!" Oliver's frame sank in obvious relief, and he rushed toward them. "Thank god."

Panic surged in Mal'ik's chest as he watched the distance between them shorten precipitously. He slung the gatlung off his back on instinct. "You shouldn't be here."

Oliver's eyes widened, and he stuttered to a stop mid-stride, as though fear of the blade warred with something else that still wanted to push him forward. He raised his hands. "Mal'ik."

"You shouldn't be here," Mal'ik repeated and finally took in the clothes Oliver was wearing. Beautiful, elegant, more formal than even his usual fare. Mal'ik was breaking out a terrorist and Oliver was dressed in luxury. Because he wasn't supposed to be here. "Go back to your banquet, Oliver."

"No, I'm not going to the stupid banquet." Oliver scowled. "I can't sit back and drink cocktails knowing what you're doing. You can't—"

"Stop." Mal'ik tightened his grip on the gatlung until his knuckles were white. He hadn't thought he would have to face Oliver, not again and not like this. "I'm not following other people's orders anymore. Even yours, Oliver."

"I'm not here to order you to do anything." Oliver took more steps toward him. And Mal'ik's heart rate jumped. He knew he couldn't use his weapon on Oliver, and it would break him to feel Oliver's hands on him one last time just to leave him. "I can't let you—"

"Oliver, stop!" He was within lunging distance of Mal'ik's gatlung now.

"I can't let you go alone!" Oliver knocked the blade away from him and was suddenly in Mal'ik's space, chest to chest, his hands on Mal'ik's jaw. "I can't let you go alone."

Mal'ik's mouth dropped open. He stared into Oliver's hazel eyes, blazing with determination. The human's hands on his face were firm. Mal'ik inhaled—nothing.

"Goddammit." Oliver let go of him with one hand and used the cuff of his shirt to wipe away the cream over his pulse points, leaving white smears on the expensive fabric.

Oliver's scent hit Mal'ik so hard it staggered him. Earth, linen, sunshine, yearning, fierce determination. Fear. So much fear, Mal'ik dropped his gatlung and wrapped his arms around Oliver without thinking, pulling him tight into his chest. Oliver shook with a suppressed sob, and the human's hands fisted into the back of his shirt.

"I've got you." Mal'ik tightened his arms around him, but Oliver shook his head and pushed against his chest.

"No. I've got you." Oliver pushed away and turned toward Sebastian. "I can help. I'm coming with you."

"No." The word was out before Mal'ik even considered it, but after a moment to do so, he repeated. "No. I can't let you do that, Oliver."

"I'm already doing it." Oliver pulled the heavy pendant from around his neck and held it out to Sebastian, but Mal'ik grabbed Oliver's wrist before the torvar could take it.

"You'd be giving up everything, Oliver." Mal'ik pulled on Oliver's wrist to make him face him instead of the torvar. Looking into those hazel eyes, Mal'ik wanted so badly to throw away his concerns and pull the human back into his chest. Oliver made him feel so powerful, not just strong, but capable and wise. The way Oliver looked at him had given Mal'ik the confidence to betray his government for the good of his people. And he couldn't repay that by letting Oliver throw his life away. "Everything you have, everything you've worked for, your father, your br—"

Oliver interrupted him with a barking laugh. "Yeah,

I'm giving up a father who's never loved me and a brother who hates me, both of whom are happy to give up the lives of however many people it takes to line their pockets."

"And have you ever been any different?" Sebastian asked before Mal'ik could respond. "I know all about you, Oliver Turner. You've been just as happy to build your wealth on the backs of whoever's low enough to serve as a foundation."

Oliver met his eyes and let out a long breath. "I won't pretend I've suddenly developed a bleeding heart. But I won't be the kind of person that sits back and lets a man I love go into danger alone when I could have gone with him."

Mal'ik's chest constricted and forced the air out of his lungs. *Love?* Was he a man that Oliver Turner loved? Him, of all the people he could have? Mal'ik opened his mouth but didn't know what words to say.

Sebastian lifted his chin. "Pretty words, but—"

"And here's my proof." Oliver yanked his wrist out of Mal'ik's shock-slackened grip. He opened the pendant on hidden hinges and pulled out a thin data strip. He handed it to Sebastian, along with his own data tablet.

Sebastian took them with a skeptical frown and inserted the strip into the tablet just as Mal'ik found his voice.

"Are you sure?" he managed. He almost reached out to Oliver, but his hands felt too clumsy in light of this new revelation.

Oliver sent him an almost cocky smile back. "Have you ever known me to be unsure?"

That startled a laugh out of Mal'ik. He shook his head. "You're the most confident person I know."

"Then you know—"

"He's coming with us." Sebastian stowed Oliver's data

tablet safely into one of his own pockets. Oliver didn't object. "I assume you have even more knowledge stowed away in that pretty head of yours."

"I do." Oliver nodded.

"Then you'd be useful as a hostage anyway."

Mal'ik spun toward him with a snarl. "He will not be a hostage."

Sebastian didn't even blink. "I didn't say he would be, just that he'd be useful—"

Alarms spun to life around them: flashing red lights and screeching sirens.

Mal'ik's world re-centered. "Follow me. Now."

He mentally kicked himself for wasting so much time, agonizing and mooning over Oliver, and took off toward the huge gates of the hangar. They would have a couple of minutes at least during which his override codes would still work before whoever had sounded the alarm put two and two together and locked him out of the system.

He skidded to a halt in front of a small transport—old enough not to stand out, new enough to be reliable. He yanked open the side door. "Get in."

Sebastian was in before he'd finished the order, Oliver hot on his heels. Mal'ik clambered in after them, then slammed the door shut behind them. When he turned to face the interior, Sebastian had already climbed into the cockpit and powered up the atmospheric transport ship with quick, expert movements.

He pushed the sliding screen toward Mal'ik as soon as he threw himself into the copilot's seat. "Codes."

Mal'ik swiped through the interface, trying to get the doors open as quickly as possible while Sebastian was already lifting them off the ground.

"Any day now. Before they lock you out of the system."

"Got it." Mal'ik hit enter and the heavy hangar doors

started sliding open with a loud grating. Mal'ik gritted his teeth. They had never seemed so slow before. Suddenly, halfway open, they stopped, and a new high-pitched shriek of an alarm pierced the air. "Fuck."

"Good enough!" Sebastian hit the throttle. They sped full tilt at the hangar doors that were now grating back closed again. "You better be buckled in back there, Turner!"

Sebastian rolled them near ninety degrees as they raced through the hangar doors, clearing them by a distance so small, Mal'ik didn't dare to think about it. Sebastian whooped, and Mal'ik—who was not buckled in—slammed his arms out to either side to hold himself steady, heart hammering in his throat. His grip held long enough for Sebastian to right them, at which point Mal'ik quickly pulled the safety straps across his chest.

Sebastian continued to gun it up and out of the perimeter of the compound, but the self-satisfied smile on his face told Mal'ik that they were as good as gone.

After several minutes, they slowed to an even cruise, low enough in the atmosphere to be below most surveillance systems.

Sebastian leaned back with a grin. "The escape is always the best part."

Mal'ik didn't reply. There was no part of anything that was happening that was even remotely good enough to be called "the best."

Except, perhaps, what Oliver had said.

Maybe Sebastian could smell him through Tesh's nose, or maybe he just had a spy's uncanny ability to read minds, but he jerked his head back toward the main compartment behind the cockpit.

"I've got it from here. I'm the only one of us who knows where headquarters is anyway." He waved his hand.

"We've got a few hours. And I promise I won't do any more rolls."

Mal'ik pressed his lips together and nodded. "Let me know if you need anything."

Sebastian shrugged. "Whatever you say."

Mal'ik was out of his seat before Sebastian finished, moving as though magnetized back to where he knew Oliver was, following the faint scent of sunshine.

Oliver sat strapped into the seat across from the door, and he looked up when Mal'ik stepped into the compartment with him. His eyes were tight, and his lower lip glistened just slightly from being worried by his teeth. Mal'ik slid the door between them and the cockpit closed and hesitated.

Oliver sat up and put his hands in his lap. "I'm sorry."

Mal'ik's heart dropped like a stone.

Oliver shook his head. "I'm sorry I forced myself on you like this. It was the most selfish way to try to stop being selfish. I want you to know I don't have any expectations of what our relationship will be going forward. I don't expect you to love me—"

"Of course I love you, Oliver." Mal'ik's muscles loosened with relief, and he crossed the room swiftly to kneel in front of the human. He smelled the fear and anxiety rolling off him and cocked his head. "Is that what you're worried about? That I don't return your feelings?"

Oliver's cheeks reddened. "Well. Yes? I did just declare my feelings rather dramatically, and we've never talked about a relationship, and we haven't known each other that long, and I'm not really the most loveable person, so…yes."

Mal'ik smiled and threaded his fingers into Oliver's soft blond hair. "I love you, Oliver."

He pulled on the back of Oliver's neck and felt all the

tension drain out of the human. He slotted his lips over Oliver's and kissed him deeply. Maybe they hadn't known each other very long, but Mal'ik had been alive for a very long time, and he'd never had anything like this.

"I love you, Oliver." Oliver let out a little mewling sound that yanked on Mal'ik's heartstrings and shot down to his groin. He kissed him again. "I love you, Oliver."

Oliver pulled back with a little laugh that had some of the wetness of a sob. "That's a relief, I guess."

Mal'ik sat back on his haunches and smiled up at the human, his heart feeling too full. He kept his hand on Oliver's knee and massaged it with his thumb. "You're really sure about this? What you're doing?"

Oliver smiled and took Mal'ik's hand in both of his own. "I am. But even if I wasn't, it's a little late to turn back now."

"We could pretend we kidnapped you."

Oliver shook his head. "Not with what's on that data strip."

"What's on it."

"All of my brother's research."

Mal'ik's thumb froze on Oliver's knee. "About the fear gas?"

"You know about it?" Oliver frowned. "You weren't at the meeting."

"Patrick told me. And Teav. It sounds awful."

Oliver scowled. "And you still decided to be on the other side of it?" He waved his hand. "Sorry. Silly question. Of course you did. You're far too good of a man, Mal'ik."

Mal'ik chuckled. "Says the man who came after me."

"Yes, well." Oliver blushed again and ducked his head. "In any case, you can see why a kidnapping ruse wouldn't work. I stole that information from my father's private

database on our family ship. The blueprints, the proto-
types, the experiments, the results, all of it."

Mal'ik blew out a breath. "And you're giving it to the
Resistance."

"Yeah." Oliver dropped his head back and looked up
at the ceiling. "Maybe I've made things incalculably worse.
Maybe it would have been better to keep that weapon in
the hands of only one side." He bit his lip. "But it was the
only leverage I had. It was the only way I could think to
convince Harrison or Serihk that I was serious before you
got away."

"They're how you found out I'd be in that hangar."

Oliver nodded. "I was terrified I'd missed you. You
can't imagine how relieved I was when you walked through
that door."

Mal'ik didn't want to revisit what he had felt when he'd
walked into the hangar to see Oliver. The overwhelming
joy and affection he felt now were much better. A war to
rival the invasion was brewing on the horizon, and yet he
couldn't stop smiling.

"I wonder what you'll look like in normal clothes."

Oliver dropped his head back down from looking at the
ceiling and wrinkled his nose. "Normal clothes?"

"You're always so dressed up. But you've left all your
money behind."

Oliver laughed. "No, I've left it with Serihk. I trans-
ferred him the entirety of my personal funds and assets,
which are considerable. They'll freeze my accounts as soon
as they've discovered what I've done, and he'll have some
tough questions to answer, but I'm sure he can manage
those."

"You thought of everything." Mal'ik smiled fondly.
That was his Oliver.

But Oliver shook his head. "I didn't think about what I'd do if you didn't return my feelings."

Mal'ik pulled him down to kiss his forehead. "Well, you don't have to."

Oliver unbuckled himself to slide onto the ground with Mal'ik and relax against Mal'ik's chest. "Thank god for that."

Mal'ik wrapped his arms around him and rested his chin on Oliver's head. "I know I shouldn't be happy right now. Not with everything that's happened and with everything that will. But I am. I'm so happy, Oliver."

Oliver tightened his arms around Mal'ik, then pulled back just far enough to look up into Mal'ik's face. "I'm happy, too, Mal'ik."

And for now, as they sped toward the Resistance on a torvar-piloted transport, that was more than enough for Mal'ik.

KEEP FOLLOWING Sebastian and witness his wild love affair with the leader of the Resistance in Book 3: The Alien Infiltrator!

The Alien Refugee

GET this FREE short story exclusively available to those on my newsletter.

HE'D SCOUR out his entire being if he knew any prayers with the power to do so.

More than twenty years before the events of **The Alien Emissary** and a few short years after the brutal Klah'Eel invasion of Southern Tava, refugees of all kinds work to build new lives for themselves on the tropical planet of Carta.

Ha'ral came to Carta fleeing the horrors of the war — both the horrors that he witnessed and the horrors that he inflicted. He became a guard and dedicated himself to becoming a new man. A patient man. A kind man. A man who would never raise a hand in anger.

Maybe even a man who might deserve the playful smiles and casually intimate touches of the handsome human pickpocket who hangs around his patrols.

But Zyk came to Carta fleeing horrors of his own and

finding out who Ha'ral used to be might be more than Zyk can bear.

A *very* steamy 20k word short story set in the Inter-species Alliances world featuring a man yearning to be better, a man yearning to heal, and a happily ever after.

Content Warning for on page violence and implied past sexual trauma.

About the Author

Eryn Ivers writes sci-fi and fantasy erotic romances about flawed men who have hot sex, feel too many things, and eventually live happily ever after.

She lives on the coast of California with her ridiculously lawful-good husband and chaotic-neutral cat.

Find her at erynivers.com, and sign up for her mailing list where you can receive free short stories, cover reveals, and book recommendations.

Also by Eryn Ivers

Interspecies Alliances

The Alien Emissary

The Alien Bodyguard

The Alien Infiltrator

The Alien Medic

Other Stories

Leech: An MM Vampire Romance Short Story